General Prisons Board Ireland

General Prisons Board (Ireland)

nineteenth report, 1896-97, with appendix

General Prisons Board Ireland

General Prisons Board (Ireland)
nineteenth report, 1896-97, with appendix

ISBN/EAN: 9783742812377

Manufactured in Europe, USA, Canada, Australia, Japa

Cover: Foto ©Andreas Hilbeck / pixelio.de

Manufactured and distributed by brebook publishing software
(www.brebook.com)

General Prisons Board Ireland

General Prisons Board (Ireland)

DUBLIN CASTLE,

26th July, 1897.

SIR,

I have to acknowledge the receipt of your letter of the 23rd Instant, forwarding, for submission to His Excellency the Lord Lieutenant, the Nineteenth Report of the General Prisons Board, Ireland, 1896-97.

I am,

Sir,

Your obedient servant,

D. HARREL.

The Chairman,
General Prisons Board,
Dublin Castle.

CONTENTS.

A 3

NINETEENTH REPORT

OF THE

JENERAL PRISONS BOARD, IRELAND.

TO HIS EXCELLENCY GEORGE HENRY,
EARL CADOGAN, K.G.,

LORD LIEUTENANT GENERAL AND GENERAL GOVERNOR OF IRELAND.

General Prisons Board,
Dublin Castle,
23rd July, 1897.

MAY IT PLEASE YOUR EXCELLENCY,

1. We have the honour, pursuant to statute, to present this our Nineteenth Annual Report on the condition of the prisons and prisoners within our jurisdiction, and with respect to the registration of criminals.

2. The course recently adopted in England, on the recommendation of the Departmental Committee on Prisons, of amalgamating the statistics of the local and convict prisons, has been followed in the tables of the Appendix to this Report. An alteration has also been made in the form of the tables of committals and expenditure in the direction of assimilating them to the corresponding tables in the English Prisons Report.

I.—LOCAL PRISONS.

3. It will be seen from the following table that the number of criminal committals of criminal prisoners to local prisons during 1896 shows a slight increase as compared with the previous year when the number fell to a lower point than had been reached during any of the other years given in the table.

Committals, &c., exclusive of Prisoners Committed under Civil Process

Years.	Number of Committals.	Daily Average No. of Prisoners.	Proportion of Daily Average to 100,000 of estimated population.	Years.	Number of Committals.	Daily Average No. of Prisoners.	Proportion of Daily Average to 100,000 of estimated population.
1844,	40,145	3,703	85	1884-85	37,803	2,573	55
1850,	42,548	4,419	93	1885-86	38,554	2,564	55
1860,	30,712	3,523	43	1886-87	40,744	2,648	54
1870,	33,761	2,718	43	1887-88	40,729	2,566	53
1874,	32,379	2,377	43	1888-89	42,704	2,848	55
1875,	38,934	2,741	53	1889-90	38,792	2,346	53
1876,	41,517	2,805	55	1890-91	40,743	2,805	55
1877,	43,641	2,885	56	1891-92	37,866	2,497	52
1878-79	43,195	2,826	58	1892-93	34,685	2,318	50
1873-80	44,058	2,822	55	1893-94	34,332	2,426	53
1880-81	40,182	2,586	50	1894-95	31,474	2,817	55
1881-82	41,092	3,111	60	1895,	30,270	2,135	47
1882-83	35,434	2,025	50	1896,	32,003	2,325	51
1893-84	35,121	2,699	54				

Bridewells.

4. The committals to Bridewells, which are not included in the table above, have also been decreasing for many years, and during 1896 numbered 1,086 males and 267 females.

Ballinasloe Bridewell was closed on the 31st January, 1897, thus further reducing the number originally handed over to the Board in 1878, from 95 to 14.

Conduct of Prisoners.

5. The conduct of the prisoners has been satisfactory, and it is gratifying to notice a gradual decrease in the percentage of prisoners punished during the past few years, as indicated by the following figures:

Year.	No. of Prisoners punished.	Percentage of Prisoners punished in total of daily average of Prisoners.
1891, . . .	3,587	117
1892, . . .	4,878	178
1893, . . .	4,436	115
1894, . . .	3,704	150
1895, . . .	2,386	87
1896, . . .	3,166	82

Short sentences.

6. The Board have in their last and many previous Annual Reports drawn attention to the great number of short sentences imposed.

During the year 1896 there were 3,494 sentences of imprisonment for four days and under, of which 663 were for a period of one day only.

7. The number of Convicted Juveniles committed to prisons still continues to decrease, as is shown by the following return :—

Years.	Under 12 Years of age.		12 to 16 Years of age.		Total.		
	Boys.	Girls.	Boys.	Girls.	Boys.	Girls.	Boys. & Girls.
1889–90,	62	5	390	68	389	70	463
1890–91,	44	6	337	53	381	71	452
1891–92,	53	—	344	65	397	65	462
1892–93,	49	2	335	79	334	75	409
1893–94,	37	1	260	81	297	83	377
1894–95,	25	5	718	54	143	59	802
1895,	20	—	307	60	377	60	257
1896,	13	6	173	17	167	23	307

Special rules for the treatment of juveniles have during the past year been brought into force in this country. A copy of these rules will be found in the appendix, see page 19.

All juveniles sentenced to one month or upwards are removed under these rules, if males to Mountjoy Prison, if females to Grangegorman Prison.

The Board are glad to be able to state that for many years past, apart from the stigma of imprisonment, no moral or material harm has happened, or can happen, to juveniles in Irish prisons, who are and have been carefully shielded from contamination by association. Satisfactory, and we believe successful, efforts from a reformatory point of view are made with the comparatively few juveniles that are committed, who are under the special care of the Governors, Chaplains, and Schoolmasters. The Prison Officers generally have shown a laudable desire to assist in these good objects as far as possible.

8. The average daily number of local prisoners in custody during the year was 2,335, and the total number of deaths was 6, a death rate of 2·56 per thousand.

Subjoined is a table of mortality among local prisoners for each year during the last seventeen years.

Year.	Daily Average Number of Prisoners.	No. of Deaths.	Rate per Thousand.	Year.	Daily Average Number of Prisoners.	No. of Deaths.	Rate per Thousand.
1880–1,	3,430	14	4·51	1888–89,	3,148	11	5·2
1881–2,	3,111	14	4·78	1889–1,	2,812	8	1·78
1882–3,	3,871	7	2·11	1890–1,	2,870	9	3·6
1883–4,	3,614	11	4·04	1891–2,	2,521	11	4·76
1884–5,	2,178	10	5·41	1892–3,	2,486	15	5·51
1885–6,	2,501	10	3·71	1893–5,	2,513	8	3·16
1886–7,	2,813	9	5·49	1894,	2,161	8	1·71
1887–8,	3,866	17	5·47	1895,	2,335	6	3·36
1888–9,	2,648	6	2·27				

Of the six deaths, one was the result of acute alcoholism, two of apoplexy, one of serous effusion on the brain, one of pulmonary consumption, and one of suicide. Four out of the six were the consequences of diseases which originated before reception into prison; and, of the other two cases, one was suffering on his admission from the effects of drink.

There were three cases of typhoid fever; the disease was incubating when the prisoners were admitted.

There was no typhus, and, although amongst the general population of Dublin zymotic diseases have been unusually prevalent, diseases of this class in the city prisons have been very few.

The number released on medical grounds has been 52. Of these there were 23 women who were very near their confinement, and 29 others, whose diseases were in 30 cases reported as having originated before reception.

9. The number of cases of insanity transferred from the local prisons to asylums was 100, an increase of 29 on the number transferred last year. As one prisoner was transferred twice the actual number of persons is 102.

Of these, 4 were sane while in prison but were found to have been insane when their offences were committed; 80 were insane on admission; 3 were imbeciles; and 4 were described as weak minded or erratic. Of the remaining 11, there are 2 reported as of "fair" mental condition on reception, but with a congenital monomania; and one of them had been previously in an asylum; 2 were "apparently sane" on reception, but one of them had been previously insane. Of the 7 whose mental condition on reception ranges from "fair" to "good," 4 developed symptoms of insanity in periods varying from 11 to 49 days; and the other 3 after longer intervals.

10. A Return, similar to that published in previous years, showing the number of visits paid to the several prisons by members of the Visiting Committees during the year 1896, is subjoined.

Prison.	Number of Meetings at which a quorum was present	Number of Visits paid by individual Members.	Prison.	Number of Meetings at which a quorum was present	Number of Visits paid by individual Members.
LOCAL PRISONS.			LOCAL PRISONS—continued.		
Armagh,	6	6	Mountjoy,	11	11
Belfast,		7	Sligo,	8	4
Carlisle,			Tralee,	1	9
Clonmel,	3	20	Tullamore,	10	4
Cork, Male,	11	10	Waterford,	2	14
Cork, Female,	8	1	Wexford,	24	19
Dundalk,	4	9	MINOR PRISONS.		
Galway,	9	14	Carrick-on-Shannon,	—	12
Grangegorman,	16	9	Drogheda,	—	1
Kilkenny,	4	9	Enniskillen,	2	—
Kilmainham,	8	18	Mullingar,	1	3
Limerick, Male,	6	19	Omagh,	1	1
Limerick, Female,	7	12	Wicklow,	4	1
Londonderry,	9	6			

It was, we regret to say, our duty to call the attention of Government to the failure on the part of the Visiting Committee of one of the local prisons to pay any visit at all for more than a year to the prison to which they had been appointed.

With this exception, the Board desire again to express their acknowledgment of the valuable assistance afforded by the Visiting Committees, and the public service rendered by them in their painstaking efforts in connection with the investigation of cases of indiscipline and misconduct.

During the past year a further extension of the provisions of the Prisons Amendment (Ireland) Act, 1884, as to the appointment of joint Visiting Committees was made and embodied in a new order, dated 22nd May, 1897, which, *inter alia,* provides for the appointment of committees once a year only, i.e., at Summer Assizes, instead of, as formerly, at both Spring and Summer Assizes, except in the case of the Visiting Committees of the Dublin prisons, who are to be appointed in the month of April each year.

11. It has been of late the practice of the Board, acting under the powers conferred on them by the 29th Section of the Act 19 and 20 Vic., c. 68, and the 17th Section of the Act, 40 and 41 Vic. c. 49, to make a deduction of the estimated cost of the prison allowance of food, not exceeding 8½d. per day, in certain cases when a prisoner, committed for begging or vagrancy, has money in possession.

In one such case a female prisoner committed for begging was found to have on her person or in the Bank property to the amount of nearly £250.

II.—CONVICT PRISONS.

12. The number of convicts in custody on 31st December, 1896, was :—

—	Male.	Female.	Total.
In Convict Prisons, . . .	344	27	861
In Local Prisons, . . .	16	—	16
Gross total of Convicts in Custody on 31st Dec., 1896, .	360	27	887

New sentences

13. The number of convicts sentenced to penal servitude during the year ending 31st December, 1890, was:—

—	Males.	Females.	Total.
3 years, ...	31	9	40
4 „	1	—	1
5 „	18	4	22
6 „	1	—	1
7 „	1	1	2
10 „	9	—	9
14 „	1	—	1
15 „	2	—	2
Death, commuted to P. S. for Life,	3		3
Gross Total sentenced during year.	67	14	81

Revocation of Licences.

14. The Revocations and Forfeitures of Licences in Ireland during the year ended 31st December, 1890, were as follow:—

—	Males	Females.	Total.
Forfeited for breach of conditions of Licence, .	8	—	8
Forfeited or revoked in consequence of a conviction for other offences, ...	22	1	23
Gross Total, ...	30	1	31

Convicts released.

15. Disposal of convicts during the year ending 31st December, 1896:—

—	Males.	Females.	Total
Discharged from Prisons:—			
On Completion of Sentence, .	—	—	—
On Commutation of Sentence,	6	1	7
On Licence, ...	122	11	133
Gross total disposed of during year, . . .	128	12	140

16. The following table shows the number of convicts Number of convicted, discharged, and in custody at intervals of five years Convicts. between 1854 and 1880-1, and for every successive year to the present time :—

TABLE showing the number of Convicts "Convicted," "Discharged," and "in Custody," in certain years since the year 1654 inclusive.

Year.	No. Convicted.	No. Discharged.*	In custody on January 1st.		
	M. and F.	M. and F.	M.	F.	Total.
1854	710	654	...	...	15,645
1855	515	620	5,597	330	5,427
1860	331	531	1,457	444	5,541
1865	290	410	1,373	364	1,578
1870	245	353	678	343	1,230
1875	941	359	368	204	1,132
1880-81	193	311	669	143	657
1881-82	202	215	694	110	804
1882-83	250	441	790	145	865
1883-84	145	201	759	83	900
1884-85	123	184	754	85	835
1885-86	99	197	700	85	785
1886-87	92	248	866	66	932
1887-88	102	162	624	54	678
1888-89	97	133	466	45	512
1889-90	88	104	426	28	454
1890-91	88	140	415	39	453
1891-92	718	147	443	37	480
1892-93	68	170	441	30	471
1893-94	108	159	446	39	485
1894-95	116	167	437	37	474
1895	102	181	437	37	474
1896	81	149	289	35	424

* Including those discharged by remission of sentence.
† In addition to this number there were six convicts under detention in the county prisons, and several approved in Bethesda and elsewhere, who were nominally still charged in Ireland.

17. The conduct of the Convicts has been generally good. Conduct of There was no case of corporal punishment during the year. Convicts.

The following return gives the particulars and percentages of Convicts punished for the last six years:—

Year.	No. of Prisoners punished.	Percentage of Prisoners punished to Total Number of Prisoners.
1891,	141	31·1
1892,	147	2·3
1893,	145	3·4
1894,	146	6·0
1895,	113	27·1
1896,	89	27·2

18. In the Convict Prisons there was one death, caused by pneumonia. Ten were released on medical grounds, and six were transferred to the Criminal Lunatic Asylum.

III.—GENERAL.

19. In Table XXIII. of the Appendix will be found the particulars relating to the industries carried on in Local and Convict Prisons. The principal Prison employments, in addition to the work requisite for keeping the prison clean and in good order, are the following:—

Tailoring.—All the warders' uniforms and prisoners' clothing are made in the prisons.

Shoemaking.—All the warders' boots and prisoners' shoes are made in the prisons.

Stone-breaking.—The chief employment for hard labour male prisoners.

Oakum-picking.—Now reduced as much as possible, but retained as a cellular employment for prisoners where more suitable work is not obtainable.

Firewood Cutting.—The firewood required throughout Ireland by the Board of Public Works is cut in the prisons, and the Prisons Department holds also several contracts for supplies to military barracks.

Mat-making.—Affords remunerative and suitable employment in several prisons.

Washing.—This forms one of the principal employments for females; but males are in certain prisons also employed. The washing of the Royal Irish Constabulary Depôt, Dublin Metropolitan Police, and of certain military barracks is done in the prisons.

Carpentry and Smithing.—Most of the requirements of the service under this heading are carried out by prison labour.

Brush-making.—All the brushes for the service are made in Mountjoy Prison.

Baking.—The bread for the Dublin and Cork Prisons is baked by prison labour.

Weaving.—All the frieze and linsey required for the prisoners' garments is made in Mountjoy Prison.

Sewing and Knitting.—The prisoners make up all the underclothing, socks, stockings, sheets, mattresses, &c., required for the service.

Mail Bag Making.—Most of the bags for the Irish Postal Service are made by prison labour.

Agriculture.—The farm of 34 acres recently acquired at Maryborough Prison is being drained, reclaimed, and tilled by convict labour, and all available ground at the other prisons is cultivated by prison labour.

Buildings, &c.—The work of reconstruction at Cork Male Prison continues to afford useful employment for a working party of convicts, averaging in number about 14 during the year, and a working party averaging about 18, has been employed at Maryboro' Prison in building a wall around the prison farm.

Gardening as a prison industry is a success from every point of view, physical, moral, and financial, especially at Maryborough, Belfast, and Tralee Prisons, where its beneficial effects on the prisoners engaged at it are very satisfactory. It lessens the number of prison offences. As it is an eminently suitable form of employment for women, special attention has been devoted to its development at the female prisons at Cork and Grangegorman.

The profit in the Manufacturing Department during the year 1896-7 amounted to £3,042 14s. 10d. This shows a decrease of £287 10s. 3d. as compared with the previous year, which is mainly accounted for by the discontinuance of carpet beating in the prisons for sanitary and other reasons, as mentioned in last year's report.

20. The greater cost per prisoner in the smaller as compared with the larger local prisons is noteworthy, especially in the matter of staff, e.g., the annual charge per prisoner for staff at Wexford, with a daily average of 37 prisoners, is £53 1s. 7d., while at Armagh, with an average of 89 prisoners, it is only £19 11s. 11d., and at Belfast, with an average of 389, it falls to £11 1s., the annual average cost of "maintenance" at the same prisons being £11 1s. 4d., £9 14s. 7d., and £8 17s. 5d., per prisoner, respectively.

21. The Board are glad to report that another Prisoners' Aid Society has been added to the list published in last year's Report, viz., The "Belfast Male Catholic Discharged Prisoners' Aid Society," which was certified on 1st August, 1896.

The following are now the existing certified Societies :—

DUBLIN :

Roman Catholic Female Prisoners' Aid Society.
Roman Catholic Male Prisoners' Aid Society.
Society for the Relief of Poor Protestants (Male and Female) discharged from Prison.

BELFAST :

Prison Gate Mission for Women (Protestant).
Prison Gate Mission for Men (Protestant).
Male Catholic Discharged Prisoners' Aid Society.

LIMERICK.

Limerick Prisoners' Aid Society (undenominational).

In November, 1896, the Commissioners of Charitable Donations and Bequests, on the recommendation of the General Prisons Board, arranged that the income from the "Barbara Tuthill" Charity, heretofore administered by the Board, in the absence of a suitable society at Limerick, should, in future, be paid to the new Society.

Much remains to be done in the way of establishment of such societies in connection with the local prisons where they do not at present exist.

22. In several cases permission has during the year been granted to lady visitors to visit female prisoners of their own religion.

IV.—REGISTRATION OF CRIMINALS.

23. It will be seen from Table XXVI. in the Appendix that the number of habitual criminals and discharged convicts registered in the year 1896, was 167, as compared with 199 in the previous year.

In connection with the new anthropometric system for identification of criminals, a series of rules as regards the measurement and photography of prisoners has been made under the Penal Servitude Act of 1891. A copy of these rules will be found in the appendix, page 115. Steps have also been taken to re-organise the photographic department of the Service, which is under the supervision of an Officer of the Staff at Headquarters, who has a special knowledge of photography. An allowance has been sanctioned by the Treasury for the taking of photographs, which will afford a stimulus to the officers employed at this work.

The particulars of habitual criminals and convicts released from prison are now published twice a week for the information of the police, in addition to being afterwards published in a yearly volume.

V.—DEPARTMENTAL.

24. Mr. A. J. Hamilton-Smythe, M. Inst. C.E., was, we regret to state, obliged, on the grounds of ill-health, to relinquish his appointment as Engineering Inspector, and has been succeeded by Mr. Max S. Green, A.M.I.C.E., who was appointed to the post by Your Excellency.

VI.—APPENDIX.

25. We beg to refer to the Appendix for Copies of Circulars Tabular Returns, and Official Reports.

We have the honour to be

Your Excellency's obedient Servants,

J. S. GIBBONS, *Chairman*.

JOHN MULHALL, *Vice-Chairman*.

STEWART WOODHOUSE, M.A., M.D.

APPENDIX

TO

NINETEENTH REPORT OF THE GENERAL PRISONS BOARD.

PART I.

CIRCULARS AND CIRCULAR MEMORANDA.

Circular No. 448.

General Prisons Board, Dublin Castle,
13th April, 1896.

The Governors (or other Officers in charge) of H.M. Prisons.

The Governor may allow a prison officer to write a letter, memorial, or other statement, on a prisoner's behalf, at the prisoner's request, if satisfied that the prisoner is unable to do so.

Either the Governor, Deputy-Governor, or the Chief Warder should be present at the writing of any such statement, and both he and the writer should sign their names at foot of the document, as witnesses that the statement was correctly taken down and read to the prisoner, and that the prisoner affixed his mark thereto (4,311).

By order,

S. H. DOUGLAS, Secretary.

———

Circular No. 450.

General Prisons Board, Dublin Castle,
22nd April, 1896.

To the Governors (or other Officers in charge) of H.M. Prisons.

I am instructed by the General Prisons Board to inform you that Circular No. 96, of 10th November, 1882, is cancelled, and to direct that in future, when prisoners are transferred from one prison to another, they shall not be required to carry their private clothes between the Prisons and the Railway Stations; but that, in cases where the prisoners are marched, the Governor shall arrange with the Police for the hiring of a car for the purpose (4,583).

By order,

S. H. DOUGLAS, Secretary.

———

Circular No. 451.

General Prisons Board, Dublin Castle,
31st July, 1896.

To the Governors of H.M. Prisons.

Referring to memo. of 29th January, 1885, on the subject of Lodging Allowances for married officers in the Irish Prisons Service whose families cannot be accommodated with Prison Quarters, the General Prisons Board have pleasure in announcing that, on their recommendation, the Lords Commissioners of Her Majesty's Treasury have decided that, in the case of officers living outside the prison, the present Lodging Allowances may, for the future, be considered as paid in lieu of Quarters only, and that a further annual sum may be paid as a cash allowance in lieu of Fuel and Light, and their Lordships have fixed this allowance:—

For Principal Warders and Clerks at £4 per annum.
For Warders   .   .   . at £3 per annum.

The following will, therefore, be the monthly rates of Lodging Allowances in lieu of Quarters, Fuel, and Light, commencing from the 1st August, 1896, inclusive:—

I. To Principal Warders, including Clerks, £1 10s. 4d. per month and to other Warders £1 10s. per month (instead of £1 6s. and £1 1s. 8d. per month respectively as hitherto) in Dublin, Belfast, Cork, Limerick, Londonderry, or Waterford.

II. To Principal Warders, including Clerks, £1 15s. per month, and to other Warders £1 3s. 6d. per month (instead of £1 1s 8d. and 15s. 2d. per month respectively as hitherto) at all other towns than the six named in No. I. (9,874).

By order,

R. LEWIS,
Clerk in Charge of Accounts.

———

General Prisons Board, Dublin Castle,
26th January, 1897.

To the Governors (or other Officers in charge) of H.M. Prisons.

Circular 63, dated 16th November, 1878, and Circular 66, dated 17th December, 1878, are hereby cancelled, and the following Circular is substituted for them.

Circular No. 452.

No subordinate male officer in the Irish Prisons Service is to **marry** without having previously obtained the permission of the Board.

When any such officer applies for permission to marry, the Governor, in forwarding the application, with his opinion, will supply the following information respecting the officer's intended wife, viz.:—name, address, native county, and character.

Every officer, after marriage, is to produce his certificate of marriage to the Governor, who will report the fact and date of marriage to the Board.

Matrons and Assistant Matrons in the Irish Prisons Service must be either single or widows. While in the Service they are not permitted to marry, and must resign their appointments before doing so (591).

By order,

S. H. DOTOLIA, Secretary.

Circular No. 453.

General Prisons Board, Dublin Castle,
10th February, 1897.

Referring to Circular No. 167, of 26th June, 1880, the General Prisons Board have to transmit herewith revised scales of travelling and personal allowances which have been sanctioned by the Treasury for Prison Officers, and which supersede the scales issued with Circular No. 167, and also Circular Memo. of 1st September, 1883.

The new scales are to take effect at once (1,288).

By order,

R. LEWIS,
Clerk in Charge of Accounts.

The Sub-accounting Officers of
the several Prisons.

[ENCLOSURE.
B

(ENCLOSURE to CIRCULAR 453.)

SCALE I.

LOCAL AND CONVICT PRISONS, IRELAND.

Scale of Travelling Allowances for Prison Officers when Absent on Duty.

Grade.	Rank.	Rate per Day and Night.	Rate per Day only (and less than 12 hours).	Railway Class.
I.	Secretary, Prison Superintendents, Chaplains, Medical Officers.	18s.	8s.	1st.
II.	Deputy Governors.	10s.	4s.	1st.
III.	Chief Warders, Stewards, Clerks, Principal Matrons, Convict Service, Matrons, Local Service, Principal Warders, Convict Service.	8s.	4s.	2nd.

		Break-fast.	Din-ner.	Sup-per.	Total Travel-ling per Day.	Rate per Night.	
IV.	Warders, Clerks, and Assistant Matrons, and all Female Officers of inferior rank. Warders and all Male Officers of similar rank, and Subsidised Keepers.	1s.	2s.	1s.	4s.	2s.	3rd.

Officers allowed 2nd Class when available, should travel 3rd Class when there is no 2nd Class.

SCALE II.

LOCAL AND CONVICT PRISONS, IRELAND.

Scale of Personal Allowances to Prison Officers while they are temporarily employed on Duty in Prisons situated at a distance from the Prison to which they are attached.

1. For the first seven days the rate per day only of Scale 1.

2. After seven days the following rates :—

For Grade   I.   :   :   :   4s. per Day.
         II.   :   :   :   3s.
         III.   :   :   :   2s.
         IV.   :   :   :   1s. 6d.

A nightly allowance is not given in above cases.

3,984

General Prisons Board, Dublin Castle
11th March, 1897.

To the Governors (or other Officers in charge) of the several Prisons.

I am directed to forward, for your information and guidance, a copy of new rules with respect to the treatment of juvenile offenders which, having been laid before Parliament for 40 days, and granted, are to be put in force at once.

With reference to rule 2, it will be your duty, on the committal of a prisoner under the age of 16, who has been sentenced for one month or upwards, to at once forward to this office his or her name, &c., on the usual form with a view to removal to Mountjoy or Grangegorman Prison.

Rule 4 (b) should be taken into special consideration when the annual demands for library books are being prepared.

Instructions will be issued in a few days as to the physical drill referred to in rule 4 (c).

The new rules should be duly brought under the notice of the Visiting Committee, and the attention of the Chaplain should be specially directed to rule No. 7.

Please acknowledge receipt, and state how many sheets of these rules you will require for posting up in the cells appropriated to juvenile offenders, and in other parts of the prison.

By order,

S. H. DOUGLAS, Secretary.

SPECIAL RULES FOR JUVENILE OFFENDERS.

By the General Prisons Board for Ireland.

In pursuance of the General Prisons (Ireland) Act, 1877, the General Prisons Board for Ireland hereby make the following Rules with respect to the treatment of Juvenile Offenders:—

1. Every prisoner under the age of 16 shall be classed as a juvenile offender, and shall be treated under the following Rules:—

2. If the sentence be for one month and upwards, he shall be located in a prison in which accommodation is set apart for juvenile offenders. If the sentence be under one month, he shall be retained in the prison to which he has been committed, but be lodged in a part of the prison where he shall be completely separated from the adult prisoners.

3. A juvenile offender shall exercise, receive school instruction, and be seated in chapel, apart from, and, if possible, out of sight of adult prisoners, with whom he shall not, on any occasion, be permitted to come into contact.

4. In the case of a juvenile offender the ordinary prison discipline shall be mitigated in the following manner:—

    (a.) He shall not be required to sleep on a plank bed.
    (b.) He shall be allowed special library books as well as books of instruction, from the time of his reception and throughout his sentence.

B 2

(c.) He may be employed in association with other juvenile offenders in work-shops, or in out-door work, such as gardening, &c.

(d.) He shall, as far as possible, be instructed in a trade which may be useful to him on release.

(e.) He shall, if medically fit, be exercised daily at physical drill in lieu of, or in addition to, walking exercise, with a view to his physical development.

5. A juvenile offender may be allowed by the Visiting Committee to receive extra visits, if, in their opinion, such visits are desirable and calculated to improve his moral welfare and future career.

6. Whenever a child under 14 years of age is committed to prison, the Governor shall report his reception direct to the Under Secretary to the Lord Lieutenant, Dublin Castle, the same day that the child is first received into custody or again received after having been brought before the court on remand or otherwise, unless by the warrant of commitment such child is ordered to be detained in a reformatory or industrial school.

7. It shall be the duty of the Chaplain to devote individual attention and care to the juvenile offenders, and, in co-operation with the visiting committee and the Discharged Prisoners' Aid Society, to make every possible provision for their protection and care on discharge.

Made and executed this 16th day of July, 1890, by the General Prisons Board for Ireland.

J. S. GIBBONS, Chairman.

[Seal.]

By the Lords Justices and Privy Council in Ireland.

HEDGES EYRE CHATTERTON.

GERALD FITZGIBBON.

In pursuance of the General Prisons (Ireland) Act, 1877, We, the Lords Justices-General and General Governors of Ireland, with the approval, advice, and consent of the Privy Council of Ireland, have settled, and hereby approve of, the foregoing Rules made by the General Prisons Board for Ireland.

Given in the Council Chamber, Dublin Castle
the 10th day of August, 1890.

W. M. JOHNSON.   WILLIAM O'BRIEN.

G. T. REDINGTON.

APPENDIX

TO

NINETEENTH REPORT OF THE GENERAL
PRISONS BOARD.

PART II.

PRISON TABLES.

TABLE I.—RETURN of COMMITTALS to the

		COMMITTED.			
PRISONS.	On Remand and afterwards Discharged.	For trial at Assizes and Quarter Sessions, and in the meantime			Otherwise disposed of.
		Tried and Convicted.	Tried and Acquitted.	Remaining in Custody at end of year.	
TOTAL, M. & F., { Local Prisons. / Convict.	1,988	877	392	96	48

MALES.

Larger Prisons,
Armagh,
Belfast,
Cork Male,
Clonmel,
Cork, Male,
Dundalk,
Galway,
Kilkenny,
Kilmainham,
Limerick, Male,
Londonderry,
Mountjoy,
Nenagh,
Tralee,
Tullamore,
Waterford,
Wexford,

Minor Prisons,
Carrick-on-Shannon,
Lifford,
Monaghan,
Mullingar,
Omagh,
Wicklow,

Convict Prisons,

| Total Males | 1,618 | 751 | 334 | 76 | 48 |

FEMALES.

Larger Prisons,
Armagh,
Belfast,
Cork Female,
Cork, Female,
Galway,
Kilmainham,
Limerick, Female,
Londonderry,
Mayo,
Tralee,
Tullamore,
Waterford,
Wexford,

Minor Prisons,
Carrick-on-Shannon,
Dundalk,
Enniskillen,
Mullingar,
Omagh,
Wicklow,

Convict Prisons,
Grangegorman,

| Total Females | 369 | 126 | 58 | 9 | 9 |

from 1st January, 1896, to 31st December, 1896.

Want of Sureties.	Naval and Military Offenders.	Remaining on Remand at end of year.	Other Classes.	On Remand to Minor Prisons and taken on remands to Larger Prisons on same charge.	Total Committals, excluding Debtors and Criminals under Civil Process.	Debtors and Prisoners under Civil Process.	Gross Totals.	PRISONS.
COMMITTED.								
685	390	71	183	233	34,126	74	34,197	Local Prisons } TOTAL M. & F.
-	-	-	3	-	3	-	3*	Convicts } TOTAL M. & F.
MALES.								
								Larger Prisons.
[illegible]	[illegible]	[illegible]	13	-	[illegible]	3	[illegible]	Armagh.
[illegible]	12	12	[illegible]	-	[illegible]	3	[illegible]	Belfast.
[illegible]	1	-	2	-	[illegible]	-	[illegible]	Castlebar.
[illegible]	10	2	-	-	[illegible]	4	[illegible]	Clonmel.
[illegible]	20	-	18	-	1,872	[illegible]	[illegible]	Cork, Male.
[illegible]	[illegible]	7	[illegible]	-	[illegible]	[illegible]	[illegible]	Dundalk.
[illegible]	[illegible]	-	4	-	[illegible]	[illegible]	[illegible]	Galway.
[illegible]	30	-	[illegible]	-	[illegible]	-	[illegible]	Kilkenny.
[illegible]	[illegible]	33	[illegible]	-	[illegible]	31	[illegible]	Kilmainham.
[illegible]	[illegible]	-	[illegible]	-	[illegible]	[illegible]	[illegible]	Limerick, Male.
[illegible]	[illegible]	3	1	-	[illegible]	-	[illegible]	Londonderry.
[illegible]	[illegible]	-	30	-	[illegible]	-	[illegible]	Mountjoy.
13	10	1	-	-	[illegible]	[illegible]	[illegible]	Sligo.
17	[illegible]	4	[illegible]	-	[illegible]	[illegible]	[illegible]	Tralee.
17	16	-	[illegible]	-	[illegible]	[illegible]	[illegible]	Tullamore.
[illegible]	[illegible]	-	[illegible]	-	[illegible]	-	[illegible]	Waterford.
[illegible]	6	1	-	-	[illegible]	4	[illegible]	Wexford.
								Minor Prisons.
-	[illegible]	-	-	18	[illegible]	-	[illegible]	Carrick-on-Shannon.
1	[illegible]	-	-	[illegible]	[illegible]	-	[illegible]	Dungannon.
-	[illegible]	-	-	[illegible]	[illegible]	-	[illegible]	Enniskillen.
1	[illegible]	-	1	[illegible]	[illegible]	-	[illegible]	Mullingar.
-	-	-	-	[illegible]	[illegible]	6	[illegible]	Omagh.
-	6	-	-	[illegible]	[illegible]	-	[illegible]	Wicklow.
								Convict Prisons.
-	-	-	-	-	-	-	-	
301	390	66	118	169	23,021	68	23,083	Total Males.
FEMALES.								
								Larger Prisons.
17	-	1	10	-	[illegible]	-	[illegible]	Armagh.
[illegible]	-	2	3	-	[illegible]	-	[illegible]	Belfast.
[illegible]	-	-	-	-	91	-	94	Castlebar.
[illegible]	-	-	[illegible]	-	[illegible]	1	[illegible]	Cork, Female.
[illegible]	-	-	-	-	[illegible]	-	[illegible]	Galway.
119	-	3	[illegible]	-	[illegible]	1	[illegible]	Grangegorman.
[illegible]	-	-	[illegible]	-	[illegible]	-	[illegible]	Limerick, Female.
[illegible]	-	1	-	-	[illegible]	1	[illegible]	Londonderry.
[illegible]	-	-	[illegible]	-	[illegible]	-	[illegible]	Sligo.
[illegible]	-	-	[illegible]	-	[illegible]	1	[illegible]	Tralee.
11	-	-	-	-	[illegible]	-	[illegible]	Tullamore.
[illegible]	-	-	20	-	[illegible]	1	[illegible]	Waterford.
[illegible]	-	1	-	-	[illegible]	1	[illegible]	Wexford.
								Minor Prisons.
-	-	-	-	[illegible]	[illegible]	-	[illegible]	Carrick-on-Shannon.
-	-	-	-	[illegible]	[illegible]	-	[illegible]	Dungannon.
-	-	-	-	[illegible]	[illegible]	-	[illegible]	Enniskillen.
-	-	-	-	11	[illegible]	-	[illegible]	Mullingar.
1	-	-	-	[illegible]	[illegible]	-	[illegible]	Omagh.
-	-	-	-	[illegible]	[illegible]	-	[illegible]	Wicklow.
								Convict Prison.
-	-	-	3	-	3	-	3	Grangegorman.
386	-	6	65	64	11,105	6	11,110	Total Females.

committed to Mountjoy Prison, and are thus counted twice. In order to obtain the total number of committals, as [illegible] in the Larger Prisons on remand charge, [illegible] should be deducted from gross [illegible].

* Convicts received back from Lunatic Asylums.

TABLE III.—Number of Prisoners in each Local and Convict Prison on the First Day of each Month during the Year ended 31st December, 1896 (at Unlock).

Prisons.	1st Jan.	1st Feb.	1st March.	1st April.	1st May.	1st June.	1st July.	1st Aug.	1st Sept.	1st Oct.	1st Nov.	1st Dec.
TOTAL { Local Prisons, M. &F. { Convicts,	2,051 518	2,240 449	2,220 401	2,293 389	2,312 382	2,438 373	2,570 357	2,529 372	2,509 376	2,360 370	2,399 376	2,394 333

MALES.

LOCAL PRISONS.
Larger Prisons.

Armagh,												
Belfast,												
Clonmel,												
Cork Male, { Local Prisoners { Convicts,												
Dundalk,												
Galway,												
Kilkenny,												
Kilmainham,												
Limerick Male,												
Londonderry,												
Mountjoy,												
Sligo,												
Tralee,												
Tullamore,												
Waterford,												
Wexford,												

Minor Prisons.

Carrick-on-Shannon,												
Drogheda,												
Enniskillen,												
Monaghan,												
Omagh,												
Wicklow,												
Total in Local Prisons,	1,563	1,665	1,826	1,718	1,709	1,734	1,800	1,877	1,806	1,874	1,865	1,845

CONVICT PRISONS.

Maryboro',												
Mountjoy,												
Total in Convict Prisons,	386	378	370	358	361	344	339	342	343	337	334	333

FEMALES.

LOCAL PRISONS.
Larger Prisons.

Armagh,												
Belfast,												
Clonmel,												
Cork Female,												
Galway,												
Grangegorman,												
Limerick Female,												
Londonderry,												
Sligo,												
Tralee,												
Tullamore,												
Waterford,												
Wexford,												

Minor Prisons.

Carrick-on-Shannon,												
Drogheda,												
Enniskillen,												
Mullingar,												
Omagh,												
Wicklow,												
Total in Local Prisons,	508	578	597	563	551	640	680	862	855	623	627	546

CONVICT PRISON.

Grangegorman,	33	50	41	33	41	40	27	41	18	43	14	33

TABLE IV. —DAILY AVERAGE NUMBER OF PRISONERS In CUSTODY, &c., &c., from 1st January, 1896, to 31st December, 1896.

NAME OF PRISON.	Daily Average Number of Prisoners, (excluding Debtors and Civil Prisoners.)			Highest Number confined at any one time about Arrest.		Lowest Number confined at any one time (both Sexes).		Highest Number of Male Prisoners confined at any one time.		Highest Number of Female Prisoners confined at any one time.		Largest Number of Male Prisoners confined at any one time.		Lowest Number of Female Prisoners confined at any one time.	
	m.	f.	Total.	No.	Date.	No.	Date.	No.	Date.	No.	Date.	No.	Date.	No.	Date.
LOCAL PRISONS.															
Larger Prisons.															
Armagh, .															
Belfast, .															
Cork, .															
Clonmel, .															
CONVICT PRISONS.															
Total in Convict Prisons.															
Grand Total,															

TABLE V.—RELIGIOUS PERSUASIONS of CONVICTED CRIMINALS committed to the undermentioned Local Prisons during the year ended 31st December, 1896, and of the Convicts in custody at end of year.

Prisons.	Established Church of Ireland.		Presbyterians.		Roman Catholics.		Other Religious Persuasions.		Total.	
	M.	F.	M.	F.	M.	F.	M.	F.	M.	F.
Local Prisons.										
Armagh,	185	61	81	3	801	281	2	–	158	21
Belfast,	918	823	687	288	1,803	1,333	3	–	8,438	2,114
Castlebar,	8	8	–	–	818	78	–	–	327	11
Clonmel,	23	–	1	–	348	–	8	–	488	–
Cork, Male,	89	–	13	–	1,848	–	5	–	1,765	–
Cork, Female,	–	88	–	8	–	397	–	–	–	1,884
Dundalk,	88	–	11	–	453	–	1	–	411	–
Galway,	17	1	8	–	818	158	1	1	838	188
Grangegorman, Female,	–	778	–	18	–	1,137	–	16	–	4,687
Kilkenny,	88	–	3	–	888	–	8	–	818	–
Kilmainham,	88	–	37	–	1,388	–	83	–	1,838	–
Limerick, Male,	88	–	–	–	1,088	–	8	–	1,878	–
Limerick, Female,	–	7	–	–	–	831	–	1	–	438
Londonderry,	118	88	83	16	788	831	8	–	988	833
Mountjoy,	888	–	18	–	8,388	–	3	–	8,878	–
Sligo,	38	10	1	–	880	148	3	–	817	188
Tralee,	13	8	–	–	888	88	–	1	838	88
Tullamore,	19	8	3	–	888	888	–	–	888	888
Waterford,	8	8	1	–	888	88	–	–	888	88
Wexford,	18	1	1	–	888	88	–	1	888	88
Total Local Prisons,	1,888	1,887	788	888	18,888	8,888	88	88	17,888	8,887
Convict Prisons.										
Grangegorman, Female,	–	8	–	1	–	88	–	–	–	87
Cork, Male,	1	–	1	–	14	–	–	–	18	–
Maryborough,	87	–	8	–	78	–	–	–	88	–
Mountjoy, Male,	88	–	18	–	188	–	6	–	888	–
Total Convicts in custody on 31st Dec.	88	5	88	1	888	88	8	–	888	87

TABLE VI.—SENTENCES on CONVICTED CRIMINAL PRISONERS committed 1896, and number of such Prisoners

(Cumulative sentences are reckoned as equal to their united length. Concurrent sentences

Prisons	Death (commuted)	Life	20 Years	18 Years	15 Years	12 Years	10 Years	7 Years	5 Years	4 Years	3 Years	2 Years	9 Years

Prisoners Committed

Criminal Prisoners other than

Local Prisons.

Armagh,
Belfast,
Cavan,
Clonmel,
Cork, Male,
Cork, Female,
Downpatrick,
Galway,
Grangegorman, Female,
Kilkenny,
Kilmainham,
Limerick, Male,
Limerick, Female,
Londonderry,
Maryboro',
Mullingar,
Naas,
Sligo,
Tralee,
Tullamore,
Waterford,
Wexford,

Minor Prisons.

Carrick-on-Shannon,
Drogheda,
Dundalk,
Nenagh,
Omagh,
Wicklow,

All Prisons,

Total,

Prisoners in Custody on

Local Prisons

Convict Prisons.

Maryborough—
Invalids,
Mountjoy Male, &c.,
Mountjoy,
Grangegorman, Female,

Total,

In addition to these there were one female and 21 male convicts confined in Grangegorman or otherwise in Prisons.

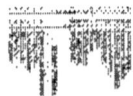

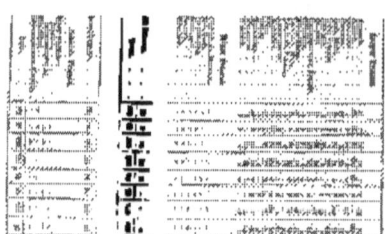

the under-mentioned Prisons during the year ending 31st December,
custody on 31st December, 1896—*continued.*

are returned as equal to one of them, or to the longer when they are of unequal length.)

				Imprisonment for						Prisons.
2 Weeks and above 1 Week	1 Week	4 Days	8 Days	2 Days	2 Days	2 Days	1 Day	Total Sentences of Imprisonment	Total Sentences	

during Year.
them Convicted by Courts-Martial.

Larger Prisons.

199	129			98	4	4		1,067	1,071	Armagh.
1,104	1,862			8	5	14	877	4,785	5,894	Belfast.
66	114			2	1	1		445	455	Cork, Male.
170	98				3			891	825	Clonmel.
249	191			104	15	14		1,055	1,502	Cork, Male.
131	134			7	3	3		1,491	1,504	Cork, Female.
121	140							486	496	Dundalk.
119	991							874	890	Galway.
679	2,691			801	24	4		4,452	4,467	Grangegorman, Female.
233	391					3		291	281	Kilkenny.
233	663			157	10	3		1,310	1,344	Kilmainham.
130	393				4			1,650	1,664	Limerick, Male.
90	143			31				241	241	Limerick, Female.
298	194			600	41			1,992	1,995	Londonderry.
118	2,691					24		4,451	4,464	Maryboro'.
110	98			24	25	14		608	617	Sligo.
119	197			1	4	1		766	766	Tullamore.
148	391		1					409	422	Tralee.
129	192	1		10	18	12		1,211	1,228	Waterford.
78	198			4	25			871	871	Wexford.

Minor Prisons.

3	79				3	1		98	95	Carrick-on-Shannon.
5	298							890	238	Dungarvan.
1	23							115	120	Enniskillen.
14	98	16		10	10			320	320	Mullingar.
	123							474	478	Omagh.
	164							470	470	Wicklow.

by Courts-Martial.

3	4			4		3		846	252	All Prisons.
4,500	9,994	37	7	2,171	183	372	603	28,349	26,891	Total.

31st December, 1896.

116	173			26	5	7	4	1,850	1,816	Local Prisons.
										Convict Prisons.
									26	Marylebone &c.
									66	Invalids.
									230	Irrespensibles, &c.
									26	Mountjoy.
										Grangegorman, Female.
111	173			26	5	7	4	1,809	2,173	Total.

TABLE VII.—NUMBER of ORIGINAL PRISONERS COMMITTED on convictions in December, 1896, and the number of previous convictions incurred by Prison under sentence—Court-Martial Prisoners excluded.

PRISONS.	Number who had previously been to any Prison											
	Once.		Twice.		Thrice.		Four times.		Five times.		Six to Ten times.	
	M.	F.	M.	F.	M.	F.	M.	F.	M.	F.	M.	F.
Larger Local Prisons.												
Armagh, . . .	91	37	43	84	53	19	43	19	21	11	63	36
Belfast, . . .	417	328	303	738	147	111	121	97	80	191	281	173
Castlebar, . .	69	1	18	1	9	1	11	1	7	1	10	4
Clonmel, . .	116	-	63	-	27	-	19	-	29	-	67	-
Cork, Male, .	308	-	134	-	129	-	71	-	39	-	131	-
Cork Female, . .	-	77	-	67	-	35	-	32	-	62	-	63
Dundalk, . .	73	-	51	-	37	-	19	-	8	-	75	-
Galway, . .	39	30	40	11	24	11	10	8	19	8	61	14
Grangegorman, Female, .	-	381	-	213	-	180	-	139	-	189	-	83
Kilkenny, . .	43	-	49	-	23	-	8	-	14	-	14	-
Kilmainham, . .	287	-	169	-	79	-	63	-	41	-	123	-
Limerick, Male, .	113	-	63	-	43	-	41	-	30	-	160	-
Limerick, Female, .	-	64	-	30	-	61	-	19	-	19	-	39
Londonderry, . .	709	10	73	6	23	9	33	7	14	5	69	60
Mountjoy, . .	673	-	379	-	234	-	189	-	133	-	444	-
Sligo, . . .	39	15	23	8	21	4	13	6	7	2	41	9
Tralee, . . .	183	39	73	14	40	9	23	1	8	1	34	5
Tullamore, . .	63	30	63	19	37	17	23	6	33	8	44	19
Waterford, . .	80	30	39	19	33	18	19	13	19	6	48	39
Wexford, . .	41	9	18	6	31	5	14	10	69	6	47	17
Minor Prisons.												
Carrick-on-Shannon,	6	2	3	1	6	1	3	-	4	1	9	1
Drogheda, . .	13	6	17	3	9	3	8	6	6	-	17	4
Enniskillen, . .	13	3	9	1	10	1	8	2	4	1	8	4
Mullingar, . .	69	6	13	4	18	4	4	1	4	3	13	7
Omagh, . . .	13	3	16	1	13	8	5	-	6	-	9	6
Wicklow, . .	39	6	79	5	18	1	9	3	3	-	4	1
Total committed to Local Prisons,	3,079	1,076	1,830	639	1,045	387	774	260	617	503	1,871	563
Convict Prisons.												
Grangegorman, Female, .	-	-	-	-	-	-	-	-	-	-	-	-
Maryborough, Male, .	-	-	-	-	-	-	-	-	-	-	-	-
Mountjoy, Male, .	-	-	-	-	-	-	-	-	-	-	-	-
Total received direct into Convict Prisons,	-	-	-	-	-	-	-	-	-	-	-	-
GRAND TOTAL,	3,079	1,076	1,830	639	1,045	387	774	260	617	503	1,871	563

Local Prisons, or direct to Convict Prisons, during the year ended 31st
such Prisoners, also the number of Prisoners who had not been previously in

under Sentence.						Number who had not been previously in any Prison under Sentence.		Total Number committed on conviction to Local Prisons, or removed thereto from Convict Prisons.		Number who when previously convicted, had for ported a Punishment of Penal Servitude or Panal Servitude.		Prison.
Seven to Twenty Years.		Above Twenty Years.		TOTAL.								
M.	F.	M.	F.	M.	F.	M.	F.	M.	F.	M.	F.	Larger Local Prisons.
39	63	160	17	532	326	595	42	798	394	12	1	Armagh.
388	226	287	415	2,372	1,879	1,968	285	3,483	2,191	32	5	Belfast.
8	4	6	9	104	22	766	48	328	84	-	-	Castlebar.
30	-	29	-	417	4	164	-	567	-	5	-	Clonmel.
143	-	189	-	1,163	-	970	-	1,633	-	21	-	Cork, Male.
-	47	-	78	-	401	-	622	-	1,684	-	4	Cork, Female.
30	-	15	-	208	-	144	-	468	-	1	-	Dundalk.
27	10	12	27	280	138	225	19	452	185	4	4	Galway.
-	390	-	1,307	-	3,795	-	272	-	4,447	-	18	Grangegorman, Female.
33	-	37	-	348	-	229	-	384	-	0	-	Kilkenny.
95	-	104	-	800	-	285	-	1,314	-	12	-	Kilmainham.
146	-	167	-	324	-	350	-	1,051	-	7	-	Limerick, Male.
-	60	-	58	-	259	-	13	-	423	-	3	Limerick, Female.
42	18	48	12	410	129	422	184	911	415	4	-	Londonderry.
438	-	482	-	3,030	-	930	-	8,369	-	50	-	Mountjoy.
37	13	18	14	272	86	283	85	393	153	5	2	Sligo.
18	1	11	11	306	68	35	37	428	69	-	1	Tralee.
13	14	7	9	299	107	262	102	664	208	7	1	Tullamore.
43	22	78	37	645	195	228	203	630	378	3	2	Waterford.
30	1	30	9	216	62	18	90	228	81	5	-	Wexford.
												Minor Prisons.
3	1	-	-	38	11	73	10	36	73	-	-	Carrick-on-Shannon.
9	6	4	-	78	30	92	38	177	58	1	-	Drogheda.
8	3	8	9	80	17	17	3	97	30	-	-	Enniskillen.
3	6	5	9	97	30	82	40	130	30	2	-	Kilkenny.
22	5	41	10	170	35	61	34	390	42	3	-	Omagh.

Table VIII.—Return of Prisoners within each of the following on the 31st

PRISONS.	Under 12 years.		12 years and under 14.		14 and under 17.		17 and under 20.		20 and under 30.	
	M.	F.	M.	F.	M.	F.	M.	F.	M.	F.
Larger Local Prisons.										
Armagh, ...	-	-	-	-	10	2	62	6	15	5
Belfast, . . .	-	-	-	-	60	2	62	12	50	15
Castlebar, . . .	-	-	-	-	2	-	5	2	3	1
Clonmel, . .	-	-	-	-	12	-	11	-	9	-
Cork, M. {Local Prisoners,	-	-	-	-	57	-	57	-	56	-
{Convicts. .	-	-	-	-	-	-	5	-	2	-
Cork, Female, . .	-	-	-	-	-	1	-	27	-	25
Dundalk, . . .	-	-	-	-	2	-	20	-	11	-
Galway, ...	-	-	1	-	7	2	54	2	9	2
Grangegorman, Female,	-	-	-	1	-	11	-	52	-	40
Kilkenny, . . .	-	-	-	-	13	-	10	-	3	-
Kilmainham, . .	-	-	6	-	17	-	22	-	25	-
Limerick, Male, . .	-	-	-	-	13	-	64	-	15	-
Limerick, Female, .	-	-	-	-	-	2	-	11	-	15
Londonderry, . .	-	-	-	-	7	-	52	2	12	11
Mountjoy, . . .	-	-	2	-	64	-	147	-	60	-
Sligo, . . .	-	-	1	-	10	2	27	1	14	2
Tralee, . . .	-	-	1	-	2	-	22	-	2	2
Tullamore, . . .	-	-	-	-	2	1	12	1	14	2
Waterford, . . .	-	-	-	-	4	2	4	2	4	12
Wexford, ...	-	-	-	-	3	-	2	2	3	5
Minor Prisons.										
Carrick-on-Shannon, .	-	-	-	-	-	1	1	1	1	-
Drogheda, . . .	-	-	-	-	2	-	2	-	6	2
Enniskillen, . .	-	-	-	-	1	-	1	-	2	-
Mullingar, . . .	-	-	-	-	2	-	1	-	-	-
Omagh, . .	-	-	-	-	2	-	2	-	2	-
Wicklow, . . .	-	-	-	-	-	-	-	-	1	-
Total Local Prisons,	-	-	12	1	222	33	600	142	220	142
Convict Prisons.										
Grangegorman, Female,	-	-	-	-	-	1	-	11	-	10
Maryborough, . .	-	-	-	-	2	-	60	-	60	-
Mountjoy, Male, . .	-	-	-	-	7	-	71	-	112	-
Total Convict Prisons.	-	-	-	-	10	1	90	11	123	10
GRAND TOTAL, . .	-	-	10	1	223	34	702	153	225	152

Periods of Age remaining in each of the Local and Convict Prisons December, 1896.

40 and under 50		50 and under 60		60 and above		Age not ascertained.		Total.		Prisons.
M.	F.	M.	F.	M.	F.	M.	F.	M.	F.	Larger Local Prisons.
3	5	2	1	2	-	-	-	50	54	Armagh.
18	13	31	5	15	3	-	-	270	81	Belfast.
1	-	3	-	2	5	-	-	13	5	Castlebar.
3	-	2	-	4	-	-	-	64	-	Clonmel.
14	-	5	-	3	-	-	-	130	-	Cork, M. { Local Prisons. / Convicts.
3	-	-	-	-	-	-	-	16	-	
-	18	-	7	-	1	-	-	-	71	Cork, Female.
7	-	4	-	3	-	-	-	64	-	Dundalk.
6	3	5	3	1	-	-	-	40	11	Galway.
-	28	-	18	-	6	-	-	-	105	Grangegorman, Female.
3	-	6	-	-	-	-	-	66	-	Kilkenny.
5	-	16	-	3	-	-	-	180	-	Kilmainham.
7	-	3	-	1	-	-	-	71	-	Limerick, Male.
-	7	-	4	-	-	-	-	-	40	Limerick, Female.
13	5	6	2	6	3	-	-	73	26	Londonderry.
80	-	12	-	38	-	-	-	820	-	Mountjoy;
3	3	4	2	3	-	-	-	67	10	Sligo.
1	3	3	-	1	-	-	-	67	4	Tralee.
6	3	6	1	4	-	-	-	61	5	Tullamore.
2	3	2	3	-	2	-	-	18	26	Waterford.
8	5	3	-	3	-	-	-	27	6	Wexford.
										Minor Prisons.
8	1	-	-	-	-	-	-	6	3	Carrick-on-Shannon.
-	-	-	-	1	-	-	-	13	2	Dungannon.
-	-	-	-	-	-	-	-	5	-	Enniskillen.
-	-	-	-	1	-	-	-	5	-	Mullingar.
-	-	-	-	-	-	-	-	4	-	Omagh.
-	-	-	-	-	-	-	-	1	-	Wicklow.
187	106	126	57	63	31	-	-	1,413	554	Total Local Prisons.
										Convict Prisons.
-	5	-	7	-	3	-	-	-	57	Grangegorman, Female.
17	-	14	-	8	-	-	-	93	-	Maryborough.
36	-	28	-	17	-	-	-	203	-	Mountjoy, Male.
53	5	40	7	25	3	-	-	344	57	Total Convict Prisons.
217	94	233	44	95	34	-	-	1,461	552	Grand Total.

D 2

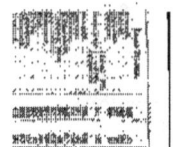

—Crimes of Convicts committed under fresh sentences... during the year ended 31st December, 1896, and ... in custody on that date.

TABLE XIV.—PARTICULARS of each case of INSANITY (amongst Prisoners)

(See paragraph 130 of Report.

Initials of Name.	Sex.			Occupation previous to Conviction.	Crime or Charge.	Date of Conviction (if convicted).	Sentence (if convicted).	Date of Discharge to a Local Prison.	No.

ARMAGH.   **LOCAL**

| P. H. | M. | 70 | M. | Shoemaker, | Stealing, | — | Remanded, | 2. 3. 96 | 1 |

BELFAST.

W. K., or S.	M.	44	M.	Labourer,	Breaking and entering,	14. 3. 94	12 c. with. h.l.	21. 2. 95	2
J. K.,	M.	25	M. W.	do.,	1. larceny, 2. malicious injury,	14. 6. 95	7 c. with. h.l.	4. 4. 95	3
J. K.,	P.	40	M.	Prostitute,	Drunk and disorderly,	24. 2. 96	1 c. with. h.l.	26. 3. 96	4
J. G.,	M.	18	R. W.	Nil,	Indecent behaviour,	14. 3. 95	1 days,	18. 3. 95	5
M. G.,	P.	43	do.	Servant,	Wounding,	18. 3. 95	To be detained in custody until the pleasure of the Lord Lieut. be known,	2. 12. 95	6
J. P.,	M.	27	Surg.	Music Master,	Assault,	17. 3. 95	1 c. each.	22. 3. 95	7
A. P.,	P.	31	R. W.	Prostitute,	Drunk and disorderly,	5. 4. 96	1 c. with. h.l.	14. 4. 96	8
F. R.,	M.	40	do.	Ironworker,	Attempted suicide,	20. 3. 95	To be kept in custody until the pleasure of the Lord Lieut. be known,	6. 4. 95	9
J. T.,	M.	10	M.	Labourer,	Theft a lock,	23. 6. 95	do.,	28. 6. 95	10
I. L.,	M.	49	R. W.	Bricklayer,	Attempted suicide,	29. 6. 95	do.,	3. 8. 95	11
A. F.,	M.	22	do.	Nil,	Assault,	16. 7. 95	do.,	2. 3. 95	12
J. O'N.,	M.	27	Surg.	Engineer,	larceny, attempt to burglary, and obstructing railway,	18. 7. 95 / 18. 7. 95	12, 12, 12, & 12 c. with penal,	27. 8. 95	13
J. G.,	M.	12	M.	Labourer,	Larceny,	2. 3. 96	6 c. with. h.l.	7. 3. 96	14
P. M'D.	M.	44	R. W.	Carter,	Using threats,	—	On remand,	15. 8. 95	15

CASTLEBAR.

P. L.,	M.	61	R. W.	Nil,	Murder,	17. 3. 96	To be kept in custody until the Lord Lieutenant's pleasure shall be known,	17. 3. 96	16
P. G.,	M.	34	do.	Labourer,	1. larceny, 2. assault,	16. 4. 96	1. 1 c. with. h.l. 2. 1 c. with. h.l.	24. 4. 96	17
J. R.,	M.	49	Surg.	Nil,	Attempting to rescind,	14. 7. 96	To be kept in custody in criminal lunatic in Dundrum Asylum till the pleasure of the Lord Lieutenant shall be made known,	4. 8. 96	18
J. M.,	M.	34	M. W.	Labourer,	Burglary,	3. 12. 96	To be kept in custody till the pleasure of the Lord Lieutenant shall be known,	28. 10. 96	19

CLONMEL.

In LOCAL and CONVICT PRISONS, during Year ended 31st December, 1896.

of Royal Commission, 1884).

No.	Mental Condition on Reception told a Local Prison.	Whether previously Insane.	Length of Imprisonment previous to that or period of Insanity, (in case of becoming in Prison).	Form of Insanity.	Supposed cause of Insanity.		Removed to Asylum. Name at time first sent Date of Removal.	Died in Prison with Date.	
PRISONS.				**ARMAGH.**					
1	Insane,	Yes,	—	Organic brain disease,	Not known,	—	Armagh, 15. 3. 95.	,,	,,
				BELFAST.					
2	Low type of Imbecile,	Not known,	3 months,	Puerperal mania,	Not known,		Belfast, 20. 1. 94.	,,	,,
3	Insane,	do.,	4 months,	Dementia,	do.,		Belfast, 3. 3. 94.	,,	,,
4	Insane,	do.,	—	Acute mania,	Chronic alcoholism,		Belfast, 14. 2. 94.	,,	,,
5	do.,	do.,	—	Delusional mania,	Alcoholism,		Antrim, 30. 5. 94.	,,	,,
6	do.,	do.,	—	Acute mania,	Not known,	New	Dundrum, 14. 3. 94.	,,	,,
7	do.,	do.,	—	Delusional mania,	do.,		Belfast, 13. 6. 94.	,,	,,
8	do.,	do.,	—	do.,	Alcoholism,		Belfast, 20. 6. 94.	,,	,,
9	do.,	do.,	—	Dementia,	do.,		Belfast, 5. 7. 94.	,,	,,
10	do.,	Yes,	—	Imbecile,	From birth,		Belfast, 2. 7. 94.	,,	,,
11	do.,	Not known,	—	Suicidal mania,	Not known,		do., 5. 7. 94.	,,	,,
12	do.,	Yes,	—	Dangerous imbecile,	From birth,		Dundrum, 24. 7. 94.	,,	,,
13	do.,	do.,	—	Dangerous moral insanity,	do.,		Dundrum, 24. 7. 94.	,,	,,
14	do.,	Not known,	—	Dementia,	Alcoholism,		Belfast, 7. 10. 94.	,,	,,
15	do.,	Yes,	—	Acute mania,	do.,		Belfast, 9. 10. 94.	,,	,,
				CASTLEBAR.					
16	Insane,	No,	—	Mania,	Self-pollution,		Dundrum, 23. 3. 94.	,,	,,
17	do.,	do.,	—	do.,	Intemperance,		Castlebar, 15. 1. 94. Dundrum, 16. 1. 94.	,,	,,
18	Not insane while in prison,	—	—	—	—			,,	,,
19	do.,	—	—	—	—		Dundrum, 10. 11. 94.	,,	,,
				CLONMEL.					
20	Showed symptoms of insanity,	Not known,	—	Delusional insanity,	Probably hereditary,		Clonmel, 23. 7. 94.	,,	,,

TABLE XIV.—PARTICULARS of each case of INSANITY (amongst Prisoners) in LOCAL

Initials of Name	Sex	Age (Years)	Education	Occupation previous to Conviction	Crime or Charge	Date of Conviction (if Convicted)	Sentence (if convicted)	Date of Reception into Local Prison	Re...

CORK (Male).

J. D.,	M.	33	R. W.	Soldier,	Military offence,	11. 4. 65	1 year and 6 a. subs. h.l.	3. 5. 67	11
J. M.,	M.	37	11.	Blacksmith,	Insubordination in Provincy Union,	21. 12. 55	1 a. with h.l.,	24. 12. 55	21
M.,	M.	50	R. W.	Labourer,	Assault, Police,	15. 64	1 a. with h...	22. 75	22
F. G.,	M.	51	do.	do.,	Indecent assault,	10. 1. 75	12 c. subs. h.l.	25. 2. 75	91
V. F.,	M.	77	do.	do.,	1. Drunk, 11. Assault, 111. Assault,	1. 1. 76	4 days, &c. &c., &c a. subs. h.l. 3 a. subs. imd.	2. 2. 76	15
F. G.,	M.	33	do.	do.,	1. Drunk, 11. Malicious damage,	22. 4. 65	1 a. with, t.h.d. 3 a. subs. h.l.	25. 4. 66	3
D. M.,	K.	71	do.	do.,	Drunk,	23. 4. 75	1 a. with, 4 in,	25. 4. 75	27
K. C.,	M.	60	do.,	Farmer,	Assault and threatening to shoot,	—	On remand,	31. 75	76
M. M.,	K.	30	do.	Labourer,	Threatening language,	1. 11. 75	1 a. with, h.l.	2. 11. 75	29

CORK (Female).

M. B.,	F.	34	R. W.	Prostitute,	Using obscene language,	2. 2. 76	1 a. with. or 11 d.,	2. 2. 76	33
M. M'C.,	F.	19	do.	Servant,	Murder,	—	To be kept in custody until Her Majesty's pleasure be made known,	2. 1. 76	51
M. F.,	F.	37	do.	Dealer,	Placing stones on the railway line,	—	To be kept in custody during Her Lord's Lieut.'s pleasure,	2. 2. 16	77
A. M.,	F.	60	No.	Housekeeper,	Larce,	—	1 a. with,	1. 1. 76	13
M. G.,	F.	30	do.	Prostitute,	1. Drunkenness, 11. Assault,	1. 4. 76	1. 1 a. with. h.l. 11. 3 a. subs. h.l.	1. 4. 76	36

BUFFALL.

| F. B. (alias J. W.) | M. | 73 | R. W. | Tramp, | Indecent behaviour, | 12. 4. 76 | 1 a. with. h.l. or 23d. | 13. 4. 76 | 99 |

GALWAY.

J. G.,	M.	33	11.	Labourer,	1. Drunk and disorderly, 11. Assaulting police,	7. 14. 76	1 a. subs. h.l.,	30. 2. 76	35
J. M.,	M.	73	R. W.	Begging,	Begging,	1. 2. 76	14 days imprisonment,	23. 2. 77	23
J. D.,	M.	63	do.	Fisher,	Violent and indecent in R.C. chapel,	4. 4. 76	7 days imprisonment,	4. 4. 76	66
M. K.,	M.	48	16.	Labourer,	Assault,	—	On remand,	4. 4. 76	85
J. M.,	M.	56	R. W.	do.,	do.,	10. 1. 76	1 a. subs. h.l.,	11. 4. 76	42
M. F.,	M.	37	do.	Pauper,	do.,	74. 2. 76	1 a. with. h.l.,	25. 4. 76	44

and Convict Prisons, during Year ended 31st December, 1896—*continued.*

CORK (Male).

CORK (Female).

DUNDALK.

GALWAY.

TABLE XIV.—PARTICULARS of each case of Insanity (amongst Prisoners) in LOCAL

Initials of Name	Sex		Religion	Occupation previous to Commitment	Cause of Charge	Date of Conviction (if Convicted)	Sentence (if Convicted)	Date of Receipt. Can Read and Write Finish	

GRANGEGORMAN.

M. R.	F.		R.W.	Rag picker	Obstructing thoroughfare		Discharged		
M. Q.	F.		R.C.	Prostitute	Riotous and drunken manner		Empties &c. &c.		
M. C.	F.		Prot.	—	Attempting suicide		1 month's imprisonment		
E. B.	F.		R.W.	Servant	Drunk		6 days or &c.		
M. B.	F.		do.	—	Assault and breaking glass		3-6 months &c.		
E. K.	F.		R.C.	None	Threatening behaviour		On remand		
R. P.	F.		R.C.	Prostitute	Attempting suicide		3 months imprisonment		
E. R.	F.		R.W.	do.	Neglecting children		1 year &c.		
M. M.	F.		do.	None	Damaging house		3 days &c.		

KILKENNY.

| J. O'B. | M. | | R.W. | Labourer | Vagrancy | | 1 mth. &c. | | |

KILMAINHAM.

M. M.	M.		R.C.	Coal porter and miner	Housebreaking		—		
P. H.	M.		R.W.	Farmer	Manslaughter		—		
W. B.	M.		R.	Labourer	Begging		—		
W. T.	M.		R.W.	Vagrant	Assault		—		

LIMERICK (Male).

W. M.	M.		R.W.	Farmer	Assault		12s. imprisonment		
J. L.	M.		R.C.	Labourer and Pensioner	Assault and larceny		do.		
J. R.	M.		R.W.	Labourer	Stealing a spade and vegetables		1 mth. or bail		
J. C.	M.		do.	do.	Wandering &c.		6 mths. imprisonment		
J. W.	M.		do.	None	Damage of Court of Glanmore	Under arrest	1 year		
J. C.	M.		do.	Labourer	Larceny		To be kept in custody during Lord Lieutenant's pleasure		
C. M.	M.		do.	Farmer	Attempt to commit suicide		To be kept in custody during Lord Lieutenant's pleasure		

and Convict Prisons, during Year ended 31st December, 1898—*continued.*

GRANGEGORMAN.

KILKENNY.

KILMAINHAM.

LIMERICK (Male).

TABLE XIV.—PARTICULARS of each case of INSANITY (amongst Prisoners) in Loca...

Initials of Name	...	...	Condition previous to Incarceration	Crime or Charge	Date of Conviction (if Convicted)	Sentence (if awarded)	Date of Removal from a Local Prison	...
				LIMERICK (Female).				
J. B.,	F.			Prostitute,	1. Drunk and disorderly, ...			
K. L.,	F.							
B. L.,	F.		R.W.					
				LONDONDERRY.				
B. K.,	F.							
W. W.	M.		R.W.	Labourer,				
				MOUNTJOY.				
T. L.,	M.		R.W.					
W.	M.			Clerk,				
T. M.,	M.			Labourer,				
F. M'V.	M.			Compositor,				
J. K.,	M.			Labourer,				
J. W.,	M.							
W. W.,	M.							
W. B.,	M.							
M. F. D.,	M.			Labourer,				
M. M.,	M.							
F. O.,	M.			Painter,				
F. M'B.	M.			Farmer,				
				SLIGO.				
F. M'L.	M.			Farm servant,				
M. M.,	F.							
				TRALEE.				
K. B.,	M.		R.W.	Carpenter,	Drunk and disorderly,			
B. K.,	M.			Victualler,	Assault and a threats,			
W. K.,	M.			Watchmaker,				

and Convict Prisons, during Year ended 31st December, 1896—*continued.*

No.	Mental Condition on Committal to Local Prison	Whether previously in Prison	Length of Imprisonment according to first sentence of Penalty (as awarded) for Crimes	Form of Insanity	Supposed cause of Insanity		Name of Asylum and Date of Removal	Died in Prison	
				LIMERICK (Female).					
53	Insane	No	—	Recurrent mania	Drink		Limerick, 24. 5. 96.	—	
54	do.	Yes	—	do.	do.		Limerick, 7. 9. 96.	—	
55	do.	No.	—	Religious mania			Limerick, 8. 12. 96.	—	
				LONGFORD & MEATH.					
56	Good	No	11 days	Acute mania	Drink		Londonderry, 22. 8. 96	—	
57	Sane	Not known	—	This man showed no symptom of insanity while in prison.	do.		Londonderry, 24. 11. 96.	—	
				MOUNTJOY.					
58	Insane	Not known	—	Melancholia	Not known		Dundrum, 25. 3. 96	—	
59	do.	do.	—	Acute mania	do.		Richmond, 21. 4. 96	—	
70	do.	Yes	—	Mania	do.		Richmond, 27. 5. 96	—	
71	do.	Not known	—	do.	do.		Richmond, 13. 6. 96.	—	
72	do.	do.	—	Acute mania with delusions	do.		Richmond, 24. 6. 96	—	
73	Not known	do.	12 days	Acute mania	do.		Richmond, 8. 8. 96	—	
74	Insane	do.	—	Religious mania	do.		Richmond, 15. 8. 96	—	
75	do.	do.	—	Primary dementia	do.		Richmond, 28. 8. 96	—	
76	do.	Yes	—	Dementia	do.		Richmond, 28. 8. 96	—	
77	do.	Not known	—	Acute mania	do.		Richmond, 14. 9. 96	—	
78	Not known	do.	28 days	Intermittent mania	do.		Richmond, 16. 11. 96	—	
79	Imbecility	Yes	—	Imbecility	do.		Richmond, 7. 12. 96.	—	
				SLIGO.					
80	Fair	Not known	14 days	Melancholia	Congenital		Sligo, 19. 5. 96.	—	
81	do.	Yes	7 days	do.	Probably congenital		Sligo, 19. 11. 96.	—	
				TRALEE.					
82	Insane	No.	—	Delusions	Not known		Killarney, 1. 5. 96	—	
83	do.	Yes	—	do.	do.		Killarney, 18. 5. 96.	—	
84	Suffering from fits, otherwise of feeble intellect	No.	Found by a jury to be guilty of the act charged, but found not to be able to act.	Imbecile	Drink		Omagh, 15. 12. 96.	—	

TABLE XIV.—PARTICULARS of each case of INSANITY (amongst Prisoners) in Local

Initials of Name.	Reg. No.	Sex.	Age.	Religious denomination	Occupation previous to Conviction.	Crime or Charge.	Date of Conviction (if Convicted).	Sentence (if convicted).	Date of Reception into Local Prison.	No.
						TULLAMORE.				
M. H.		M.	42	R. C.	Farmer	Murder	4. 12. 06	To be detained during Her Majesty's pleasure	23. 2. 24	
T. C.		M.	58	do.	do.	do.	9. 2. 95	do.	14. 3. 06	
P. C.		M.	64	do.	do.	do.	9. 2. 95	do.	19. 3. 06	
M. F.		M.	90	do.	Labourer	Attempted suicide	8. 3. 92	do.	19. 3. 06	
						WATERFORD.				
P. B.		M.	48	D. W.	Labourer					
L. K.		M.	57	do.	do.					
H. McG.		F.	39	R. W.	Housekeeper					
E. B.		F.	42	Prot.	Prostitute	Larceny	13. 6. 06	3 mths.		
P. Do.		do.	do.	do.	do.					
M. C.		M.	42	R. W.	Workman					
M. F.		M.	39	D.	Labourer	Vagrancy				
S. M.		M.	47	R. W.	do.	Vagrancy				
						WEXFORD.				
E. C.		M.	21	R. W.	Labourer	Burglary and larceny		—		
P. M.		F.	42	Ch.	Servant	Begging				
F. W.		F.	54	do.	Nurse	Assault				
T. M.		F.	38	R. W.	do.	do.				
J. Mc.		M.	42	do.	Carpenter	Vagrancy				
M. P.		M.	63	R. W.	Labourer	Assault				
						ENNISKILLEN.				**(Minor**
P. O'B.		M.	60	Ch.	Not known	Drunkenness				
						MARYBOROUGH.				**CONVICT**
W. McG.		M.		R.	Farmer	Murder of his wife				
J. S.		M.		R. W.	Labourer					
						MOUNTJOY.				
L. J. B.		M.	48	R. W.		Larceny				
G. C.		M.	27	R. C.	Labourer	Robbery				
M. F.		M.	39	R. W.	Seaman					
F. S.		M.	16	R. W.	Labourer	Assault and robbery				

and Convict Prisons, during Year ended 31st December, 1893—*continued.*

	Mental Condition on Reception into a Local Prison.	Whether previously Insane.	Length of Imprisonment previous to and symptoms of Insanity (or cause or insanity in Prison).	Form of Insanity.	Supposed cause of Insanity.	Terminations of Case.		
						Removal to Asylum. Name of Asylum and Date of Removal.	Disch. in Prison, with Prob.	

TULLAMORE.

WATERFORD.

WEXFORD.

Prisons.)

ENNISKILLEN.

PRISONS.

MARYBOROUGH.

MOUNTJOY.

Appendix to Nineteenth Report of the

TABLE XV.—RETURN OF RESTRAINTS, PRISON OFFENCES, and PUNISHMENTS

(As required by section 13

(See paragraph 93 of Report

Prisons.	Number of Cases of Restraints.		Prison Punishments.						(a) Total number of Prisoners punished.	
	Irons (Hand-cuffs).	Muffs with Straps or Strait-jacket Jackets.	Punishment Cells.		Dietary Punishment.		Loss of Stage (Days or Privilege).			
	M.	F.	M.	F.	M.	F.	M.	F.	M.	F.	M.	F.
Total M. & F.,	10	108		165		8,923		789		2,599	
Larger Local Prisons.											
Armagh,	—	—									
Belfast,	—	—									
Castlebar,	—	—	1	—	—	—	41	8	—	—	87	6
Clonmel,	—	—	1	—	—	—	125	—	6	—	167	—
Cork { Local Prisoners	—	—	14	—	31	—	494	—	172	—	814	—
Male, { Convicts,	—	—	—	—	—	—	4	—	—	—	8	—
Cork Female,	—	—	—	1	—	9	—	110	—	20	—	763
Dundalk,	—	—	3	—	1	—		—	45	—	98	—
Galway,	—	—	—	1	2	—	61	14	6	8	67	13
Grangegorman,	—	—	—	16	—	10	—	180	—	2	—	188
Kilkenny,	—	—	1	—	3	—	281	—	170	—	183	—
Kilmainham,	—	—	6	—	—	—	191	—	43	—	192	—
Limerick Male,	—	—	1	—	24	—	312	—	80	—	210	—
Limerick Female,	—	—	—	14	—	1	—	46	—	5	—	47
Londonderry,	—	—	1	1	3	—	129	5	—	—	131	5
Mountjoy,	1	—	6	—	6	—	319	—	88	—	172	—
Sligo,	—	—	6	1	—	—	316	—	81	1	85	1
Tralee,	—	—	1	—	9	—	197	1	17	1	128	1
Kilkenny,	—	—	1	—	—	1	30	14	17	3	143	13
Waterford,	—	—	3	—	1	—	92	11	—	1	14	8
Wexford,	—	—	5	—	—	—	63	15	6	5	63	7
Minor Prisons.											
Carrickon-Shannon,	—	—	1	—	—	—	—	—	—	—	—	—
Drogheda,	—	—	1	1	—	—	—	—	—	—	—	—
Enniskillen,	—	—	1	—	—	—	2	—	—	—	3	—
Mullingar,	—	—	—	—	—	—	2	—	—	—	3	—
Omagh,	—	—	—	—	3	—	9	1	—	—	11	1
Wicklow,	—	—	—	—	—	—	—	—	—	—	—	—
TOTAL LOCAL PRISONS,	1	—	60	49	98	44	8,156	568	277	51	1,587	515
Convict Prisons.											
Grangegorman,	1	—	—	1	—	7	—	6	—	—	96	8
Maryborough,	4	—	6	—	10	—	30	—	4	—	62	—
Mountjoy,	—	—	—	—	33	—	195	—	40	—		

in Local and Convict Prisons from 1st January, 1896, to 31st December, 1896.
of 40 & 41 Vict., cap. 49.)
of Royal Commission, 1884.)

(a) Number of Prisoners not punished.		Total number of Prisoners during the Year. (Columns 3 & 4).		Prison Offences.										Prisons.
				Violence.		Escapes and Attempts to Escape.		Idleness.		Other Breaches of Regulations.		Total Offences.		
32,886		27,697		193		—		1,805		4,839		6,875		Total M. & F.
M.	F.	M.	F.	M.	F.	M.	F.	M.	F.	M.	F.	M.	F.	Larger Local Prisons:
781	511	801	501	7	4	—	—	117	1	113	51	212	56	Armagh.
4,500	2,243	4,506	2,834	7	4	—	—	113	48	403	148	337	100	Belfast.
803	94	442	100	—	—	—	—	34	—	41	3	74	8	Cavan.
830		747	—	3	—	—	—	23	—	107	—	143	—	Clonmel.
1,631	—	3,149	—	1	—	—	—	257	—	601	—	859	—	Local Prisoners \} Cork
60	—	92	—	—	—	—	—	—	—	1	—	7	—	Convict. \} Male.
7	1,107	—	1,332	—	6	—	—	—	19	—	911	—	930	Cork Female.
375	—	479	—	1	—	—	—	87	—	815	—	211	—	Dundalk.
394	167	541	176	—	5	—	—	40	1	84	17	68	10	Galway.
643	—	765	—	8	—	—	1	136	9	238	—	428	—	Grangegorman—
													120	Kilmeny.
3,118	—	3,509	—	12	—	—	—	86	—	253	—	471	—	Kilmainham.
1,452	—	1,891	—	—	—	—	—	290	—	113	—	653	—	Maryboro' Male.
—	301	—	539	—	4	—	—	—	1	87	13	78	18	Limerick Female.
579	450	1,207	450	—	—	—	—	45	9	148	—	200	—	Londonderry.
2,501	—	4,445	—	11	—	—	—	45	—	230	—	324	—	Mountjoy.
342	187	648	283	1	—	—	1	45	—	192	—	247	1	Sligo.
103	113	391	116	—	—	—	—	117	—	87	1	214	1	Tralee.
540	348	712	250	1	—	—	—	201	—	156	28	401	30	Tullamore.
701	437	581	416	1	4	—	—	8	1	10	18	204	14	Waterford.
213	64	343	104	—	—	—	—	63	3	60	17	134	15	Wexford.
														Minor Prisons.
121	91	121	91	—	—	—	1	—	—	—	—	—	—	Carrick-on-Shannon.
252	65	252	90	—	—	—	—	—	—	1	—	1	1	Drogheda.
123	91	123	91	1	—	—	—	1	—	1	—	3	1	Enniskillen.
253	83	259	83	—	—	—	—	—	—	8	—	8	—	Mullingar.
299	66	311	66	—	—	—	—	8	1	1	—	11	1	Omagh.
154	30	165	30	—	—	—	—	8	—	7	—	6	—	Wicklow.
40,206	11,031	24,892	11,964	94	84	—	—	1,794	75	3,174	979	5,905	964	Total Local Prisons.
														Convict Prisons.
—	41	—	45	—	1	—	—	—	—	—	18	—	14	Grbitsgrovernwt.
116	—	148	—	3	—	—	—	3	—	54	—	57	—	Maryborough.
1039	—	471	—	40	—	—	—	5	—	803	—	310	—	Mountjoy.
604	41	473	45	45	1	—	—	4	—	277	19	327	14	Total Convict Prisons.
22,786	11,052	24,422	11,674	139	85	—	—	1,798	75	3,451	998	5,897	968	Grand Total.

TABLE XVI.—OFFENCES and COMMITMENTS of JUVENILES, *i.e.*, PRISONERS under 15 years of age, from 1st JANUARY, 1896, to 31st December, 1896 (included in foregoing Tables).

Prisons.	Convictions							Not Convicted and Untried		Total Number of Committals
	At Assizes and Quarter Sessions		Summarily		Reformatory Discharged	Total Convicted				
	Under 12 Years	12 and under 15 Years	Under 12 Years	12 and under 15 Years	Total under 15 Years	Under 12 Years	12 and under 15 Years	Under 12 Years	12 and under 15 Years	Under 12 Years	12 and under 15 Years
TOTAL, M. & F.	2	14	15	175	—	18	189	17	86	35	275

MALES.

Larger Prisons.

Armagh, Belfast, Castlebar.

Clonmel, Cork Male, Dundalk.

Galway, Kilkenny, Kilmainham.

Limerick Male, Londonderry, Maryboro'.

Sligo, Tralee, Tullamore.

Waterford, Wexford.

Minor Prisons.

Carrick-on-Shannon, Drogheda.

Enniskillen, Mullingar.

Omagh, Wicklow.

| Total Males. | 1 | 14 | 15 | 180 | — | 16 | 172 | 17 | 75 | 33 | 250 |

FEMALES.

Larger Prisons.

Armagh, Belfast, Castlebar.

Cork Female, Galway, Grangegorman.

Limerick Female, Londonderry, Sligo.

Tralee, Tullamore.

Waterford, Wexford.

Minor Prisons.

Carrick-on-Shannon, Drogheda.

Enniskillen, Mullingar.

Omagh, Wicklow.

| Total Females. | 1 | 3 | 2 | 15 | — | 3 | 17 | — | 6 | 5 | 25 |

No. XVII.—SENTENCES ON JUVENILE PRISONERS COMMITTED from the 1st January, 1896, to 31st December, 1896.

MALES.

FEMALES.

TABLE XVIII.—CONDITION of JUVENILES as to

Prisons.	Education on Committal.							
	Neither Read nor Write.		Read or Read and Write Imperfectly.		Read and Write Well.		Superior Instruction.	
	Under 16 years.	16 and under 18 years.	Under 16 years.	16 and under 18 years.	Under 16 years.	16 and under 18 years.	Under 16 years.	16 and under 18 years.
Total, M. & F.,	14	76	15	96	6	96	-	4

MALES.

Prisons.								
Armagh.	1	1	6	10	3	4	-	-
Belfast.	-	1	-	3	-	16	-	-
Carrickfergus.	-	-	-	-	-	1	-	-
Clonmel,	1	7	3	-	1	11	-	-
Cork Male,	-	3	1	-	2	7	-	-
Dundalk,	-	1	-	2	-	-	-	-
Galway,	-	-	-	-	-	-	-	-
Kilkenny,								
Mountjoh.	7	50	4	44	-	50	-	4
Limerick, Male,	3	3	3	-	-	11	-	-
Londonderry,	-	4	-	5	1	8	-	-
Monaghan,	-	-	-	-	-	-	-	-
Sligo,	1	1	-	1	-	1	-	-
Tralee,	-	1	-	-	-	-	-	-
Tullamore,	-	1	-	-	-	-	-	-
Waterford,	-	1	-	4	-	-	-	-
Wexford,	-	3	-	1	-	4	-	-
Minor Prisons.								
Carrick-on-Shannon.	-	3	-	-	-	-	-	-
Drogheda,	-	-	1	3	-	-	-	-
Enniskillen,	-	-	-	-	-	-	-	-
Mullingar,	-	1	-	-	-	4	-	-
Omagh,	1	1	-	-	-	5	-	-
Wicklow,	-	-	-	2	-	-	-	-
Total Males,	13	61	13	86	8	87	-	4

FEMALES.

Prisons.								
Armagh,	-	1	-	1	-	1	-	-
Belfast,	-	1	-	-	-	-	-	-
Carrickfergus,	-	-	-	-	-	-	-	-
Cork Female,	-	-	-	-	-	1	-	-
Galway,	-	1	1	1	-	-	-	-
Grangegorman,	-	1	1	1	-	-	-	-
Limerick, Female,	-	-	-	-	-	-	-	-
Londonderry,	-	1	-	-	-	-	-	-
Sligo,	-	-	-	-	-	-	-	-
Tralee,	1	1	-	3	-	-	-	-
Tullamore,	-	-	-	-	-	-	-	-
Waterford,	-	1	-	1	-	-	-	-
Wexford,	-	-	-	-	-	-	-	-
Minor Prisons.								
Carrick-on-Shannon,	-	-	-	-	-	-	-	-
Drogheda,	-	-	-	-	-	-	-	-
Enniskillen,	-	-	-	-	-	-	-	-
Mullingar,	-	-	-	-	-	-	-	-
Omagh,	-	-	-	-	-	-	-	-
Wicklow,	-	-	-	-	-	-	-	-
Total Females,	1	15	2	6	-	9	-	-

EDUCATION and RELIGION in 1896.

Protestant Episcopalians of Ireland		Presbyterians.		Roman Catholics.		Other Religions.		Total.		Prisons.
Under 16 years.	16 and under 30 years.	Under 16 years.	16 and under 30 years.	Under 16 years.	16 and under 30 years.	Under 16 years.	16 and under 30 years.	Under 16 years.	16 and under 30 years.	
4	51	5	18	20	330	–	2	36	275	Total, M. & F.

MALES.

–	14	–	–	–	4	–	–	–	5	Armagh.
1	–	4	2	4	10	–	–	9	34	Belfast.
–	–	–	–	–	5	–	–	–	3	Clonmel.
–	–	–	–	2	16	–	–	2	18	Cork, Male.
–	–	–	–	1	3	–	–	1	4	Dundalk.
–	–	–	–	–	8	–	–	–	8	Galway.
–	–	–	–	–	2	–	–	–	5	Kilkenny.
–	5	–	–	11	30	–	2	11	47	Kilmainham.
–	4	–	4	2	14	–	–	2	14	Limerick, Male.
1	1	–	4	1	6	–	–	2	14	Londonderry.
–	–	–	–	1	23	–	–	1	24	Mountjoy.
–	–	–	–	1	4	–	–	1	4	Sligo.
–	–	–	–	–	2	–	–	–	7	Tralee.
–	1	–	–	–	–	–	–	–	1	Tullamore.
–	1	–	–	–	4	–	–	–	5	Waterford.
–	–	–	–	–	8	–	–	–	–	Wexford.
										Minor Prisons.
–	–	–	–	–	4	–	–	–	4	Carrick-on-Shan.
1	–	–	–	–	24	–	–	1	5	Drogheda.
–	–	–	–	–	–	–	–	–	–	Enniskillen.
–	–	–	–	–	–	–	–	–	–	Mullingar.
–	1	–	–	–	6	–	–	1	8	Omagh.
–	–	–	–	–	6	–	–	–	2	Wicklow.
4	27	5	13	22	209	–	2	32	250	Total Males.

FEMALES.

–	1	–	–	–	9	–	–	–	9	Armagh.
–	1	–	–	–	–	–	–	–	9	Belfast.
–	–	–	–	–	1	–	–	–	1	Castlebar.
–	–	–	–	–	–	–	–	–	–	Cork, Female.
–	–	–	–	–	–	–	–	–	–	Galway.
–	1	–	–	2	7	–	–	2	8	Grangegorman.
–	–	–	–	–	1	–	–	–	3	Limerick, Female.
–	–	–	–	–	1	–	–	–	1	Londonderry.
–	–	–	–	–	–	–	–	–	9	Sligo.
–	–	–	–	1	1	–	–	1	1	Tralee.
–	–	–	–	–	–	–	–	–	–	Tullamore.
–	1	–	–	–	9	–	–	–	9	Waterford.
–	1	–	–	–	–	–	–	–	–	Wexford.
										Minor Prisons.
–	–	–	–	–	–	–	–	–	–	Carrick-on-Shan.
–	–	–	–	–	–	–	–	–	–	Drogheda.
–	–	–	–	–	–	–	–	–	–	Enniskillen.
–	–	–	–	–	–	–	–	–	–	Mullingar.
–	–	–	–	–	–	–	–	–	–	Omagh.
–	–	–	–	–	–	–	–	–	–	Wicklow.
–	4	–	–	3	21	–	–	3	25	Total Females.

TABLE XIX.—RETURN of COMMITTALS, &c., to BRIDEWELLS

	Number in custody at O'clock on 1st January, 1858.		On remand and afterwards discharged, committed to larger Prisons, or otherwise disposed of.		\multicolumn{10}{c	}{Number of Prisoners committed during year.}
BRIDEWELLS.					\multicolumn{10}{c	}{Under sentence of}
					12 Hours.		24 Hours and above 12.		48 Hours and above 24.		72 Hours and above.		7 Days and above 72 Hours.	
	M.	F.	M.	F.	M.	F.	M.	F.	M.	F.	M.	F.	M.	F.
Bailieborough,	1	—	26	4	—	—	2	—	27	2	—	—	—	4
Ballina, .	2	—	37	4	—	—	4	—	9	—	45	15	—	—
Ballinasloe,	—	1	28	2	—	—	31	1	21	2	19	13	—	—
Bantry, .	—	—	18	3	—	—	—	—	—	—	—	—	—	—
Cahirciveen,	3	—	19	2	2	—	3	1	22	2	—	—	—	—
Clifden, .	1	—	6	3	—	—	4	—	18	4	—	—	—	—
Fermoy,	—	1	34	44	—	—	—	—	—	—	8	4	16	7
Kilrush, .	—	—	26	1	—	—	—	—	18	4	—	—	—	—
Letterkenny,	—	—	4	—	—	—	13	1	2	1	—	—	—	—
Longford,	1	—	27	1	—	—	—	—	4	1	8	8	1	—
Macroom, .	3	—	35	—	—	—	2	—	2	1	8	—	—	—
New Ross,	3	—	24	2	—	—	1	1	2	1	—	—	—	—
Newry,	—	2	43	2	—	—	—	1	68	4	—	—	2	1
Parsonstown,	1	1	65	9	—	—	2	2	6	—	1	—	64	17
Youghal,	—	—	17	2	—	—	—	—	—	—	—	—	—	—
Total,	18	7	486	102	2	—	43	7	170	28	70	42	111	36
Ennis Lock-Up,	3	—	14	4	—	—	—	—	—	—	—	—	—	—
Grand Total,	18	7	426	104	2	—	43	7	170	34	75	42	111	36

and Lock-Up at Exits during the Year 1886.

Number of direct Committals during year.		Number received on way to larger Prisons.		Number otherwise received.		Total number of Prisoners received.		Greatest number of persons confined by ordinary at any one time during whole period.		Daily Average number in custody.		Number in custody at Lock-Up on First December, 1886.	
M.	F.	M.	F.	M.	F.	M.	F.	M.	F.	M.	F.	M.	F.
45	7	—	—	—	—	48	7	9	1	·43	·08	—	—
94	19	28	10	—	—	145	30	9	3	·58	·25	1	—
39	13	7	—	—	—	86	19	5	3	·51	·12	—	1
18	3	1	—	—	—	13	8	3	3	·22	·08	—	—
39	4	9	—	1	—	23	4	9	1	·40	·01	1	—
17	7	11	1	—	—	98	3	3	2	·28	·04	—	—
84	48	41	17	—	—	138	59	9	6	1·91	·28	1	—
34	7	—	—	—	—	33	7	9	1	·36	·03	—	—
38	3	—	—	1	—	17	3	2	7	·38	·08	—	—
34	13	3	4	—	—	43	17	9	3	·66	·13	—	—
73	7	37	2	—	—	138	19	6	3	·48	·04	—	—
33	4	9	2	—	—	34	6	3	1	·34	·03	—	—
146	13	4	8	3	—	161	16	4	3	·34	·12	—	—
138	23	14	3	—	—	173	40	13	3	3·43	·30	6	1
17	3	—	—	—	—	37	3	5	3	·35	·73	—	—
393	100	193	79	4	—	1,033	730	—	—	9·03	1·37	6	3
14	3	—	1	—	—	14	7	3	3	·33	·08	3	—
370	193	143	73	4	—	1,033	737	—	—	6·48	3·03	7	9

TABLE XX.—RETURN of the STAFF of the undermentioned PRISONS and BRIDEWELLS on 31st December, 1896, including vacancies.

PRISON.	MALE OFFICERS.							FEMALE OFFICERS.					Total.	
													Male.	Female.

(table data largely illegible)

Total, 1896,	81	27	48	81	14	263	5	3	14	38	19	421	172	
Total, 1895,	79	27	49	81	14	266	6	3	14	34	19	405	157	

* Some of the officers enumerated in the table above appendix Grangegorman and Mountjoy are also attached the District Prisons at these places.

TABLE XXI.—Escapes from Prisons and Bridewells from 1st January, 1896, to 31st December, 1896.

Prisons, &c., from which Escapes were effected.	Initials of Name.	Sex.	Age.	Date.	Offences of which convicted or charged.	Tried or Denied.	Whether separately or with others.	Whether retaken or not.
Ballina Bridewell,	J. H.,	M.	21	12.3.96.	I. Assault, II. Drunk and disorderly, III. Assault.	Tried,	Separately,	Yes,

TABLE XXII.—Works of Reconstruction, Repairs, &c., by Contract and by Prison Labour, during the Year ended 31st December, 1896.

LARGER LOCAL PRISONS.

Prisons.	Labour (Contract or Prison).	Detail of Works.
Armagh,	Contract,	[illegible]
Do.,	Prison,	[illegible]
Belfast,	Contract,	[illegible]
Do.,	Prison,	[illegible]
Clonmel,	Contract,	[illegible]
Do.,	Prison,	[illegible]

TABLE XXII.—WORKS OF RECONSTRUCTION, REPAIRS, &c.—continued.

Prisons	Labour [Convict or Prison]	Detail of Works
Cork Male,	Contract,	Nil.
Do.,	Prison,	Converting part of old quarters for officers, No. 8 block, into a church, 2 bath-rooms, and 27 cells for prisoners; fitting up 8 baths of part of right wing, male prison, and supplying with hot and cold water; replacing roof light in bath-room of Governor's house; re-seating benches in laundry; general repairs, including painting, glazing, plumbing, masonry, and carpentry throughout the prison.
Cork Female,	Contract,	Fixing a new range in penitentiary quarters; coping and connecting loose circular walls; fixing a new iron boiler in washhouse; repairing range in officers' mess kitchen; repairing roofs of prison, including 3 new ranges of lead gutters, and repairs to slating, tiling, chimneys, and water tanks.
Do.,	Prison,	Forming 3 new windows in laundry—frames, sashes, &c., being made in Cork Male Prison; fixing a new stone table in kitchen; making new bedsteads and new boards for relief of prisons; re-laying gutters of sewer pipes, back of workhouse; whitewashing, painting, glazing, and repairs to gongs and W.C.'s throughout the prison.
Dundalk,	Contract,	Re-setting mantels in steam boiler; re-setting fire-grate and mantel-piece in Governor's office; fitting up new bell between central hall and hospital; re-setting and painting kitchen grates; washing and painting ceilings in front of prison; fixing up new water-tap with B.P. cock in washhouse; supplying pipes to hot water pipes; repairing roof of prison with new slates; repairing drain pump.
Do.,	Prison,	Fixing 2 new cog wheels to crank pump; fitting up white enamelled dog sink in Governor's kitchen; laying down new concrete water course to cookhouse yard; cleaning gas mains and connections; repairing bath in Governor's house, and fitting up trap door and frame in ceiling; repairing stone boiler and cooking pans; general repairs in iron and water pipes, carpentry, painting, glazing, &c., throughout the prison; painting of woodwork and whitewashing of cells.
Galway,	Contract,	Laying gas and water pipes from male side of prison to female prison, hospital having been disconnected by the removal of old town prison; completing 2 wardens' cottages.
Do.,	Prison,	Repairing Governor's house, including roof and chimneys; putting in 8 new sash frames; papering walls of 6 rooms and repainting and colouring ceilings; cleaning and colouring walls and ceilings of hall, passages, &c., and cleaning and painting woodwork; papering and painting sundry matrons' rooms; cleaning and colouring walls of chapel, and painting woodwork; completing removal of walls of old town prison, and forming new entrance to hospital of female prison; rebuilding 30 yards of boundary wall, and forming gateway at wardens' cottages; repairing 12 store sheds, and forming water course from filters; fire-proofing wall of cell; and corridors, and painting woodwork and ironwork.
Grangegorman,	Contract,	Reglazing, leadlighting, and painting skylights of new hall; repairing and painting skylights of laundry and store room; repairing the slating, pavement, and glazing of roofs; repairing roofing of chimneys; stripping and painting gutters of new hall; cleaning and whitening ceilings of some storehouse quarters; fixing leading boiler of new bath with new flanges and connections; cleaning floors of drying closets through the prison and laundry; fixing two stocks and bars in cooking ranges, and boilers of kitchen and laundry; cleaning windows of front building.

TABLE XXII.—WORKS OF RECONSTRUCTION, REPAIRS, &c.—continued.

Prison.	Labour (Contract or Prison).	Detail of Works.
Grangegorman,	Prison,	Taking down wooden cell in hospital, and repairing wells; repairing seven doors of matron's quarters, and fitting with new locks; fitting mess kitchen boiler with new copper connections, and repairing various work of boiler house; making partition in prison kitchen and hospital, and painting same; carpentry, &c. for necessary repairs to out-offices; masonry, plumbing, gasfitting, glazing, and bellhanging.
Kilkenny,	Contract,	Erecting barb-wire fencing on wall enclosing prison garden; fencing a open piece of ground adjacent to chief warder's house with barbed wire; fixing incandescent lights in each wing of prison, mess hall, surgery, (Governor), chief warder's, and clerk's offices; repairing electric bells, crank pump, weighbridge, and gas fittings; repairing hot and cold water pipes in connection with cistern; baths; fixing set of new fire blocks in range of Governor's kitchen.
Do.,	Prison,	Putting down new floor in infant tests; fixing mantle-piece and painting and graining door; making thirty-seven new cell stools; fixing new steel-cut counters in surgery; repairing crank-pump and small hand-pump; repairing closet-cisterns, hot and cold water pipes, gas pipes, fittings, &c.; putting up mantel-pieces and repairing wood work of officers' quarters; repairing and cleaning chimneys; repairing plank beds, cell-stools, shelves, &c.; painting, whitewashing, and putting in glass in various portions of the prison; repairing roofs, &c.
Birmingham,	Contract,	Painting and papering drawing-room in Governor's house; repairing sashes in Deputy Governor's quarters, and in officers' mess. Fixing new boiler in kitchen range in Governor's house; altering position of boiler in prison kitchen.
Do.,	Prison,	Converting two old sheds into an officers' recreation room; painting office and officers' mess; repairing two back gates of prison; putting three dozen ventilators in cells in "A" and "B" wings. Repairing water and steam pipes; putting up new skylight in "B" wing; colouring and painting prison cottages and Deputy Governor's house, and repairing roofs of same; covering portion in stone-yard with slates; general repairs in painting, fixing, plumbing, pointing, and carpentry throughout the prison; commencing erection of new stores in concrete.
Limerick Male,	Contract,	Papering four rooms, hall, staircase, and ballroom in Governor's house and painting woodwork of dining room.
Do.,	Prison,	Repairing roofs of prison, gate quarters, and Governor's house, including cleaning gutters, &c.; making new grate and hearth in treasurer's house; forming mild boiler, and painting porch and windows; fitting up glass shelf in mess kitchen; fixing up tool house and sentry box in stone-yard; erecting railing round prison garden; repairing crank pump; fixing plates on cell doors to protect locks; fixing 3 new E. P. coals for water supply to reception baths; putting down concrete paths in front of wood sheds and store shed; general repairs to buildings including carpentry, plumbing, plastering, painting, glazing, whitewashing, &c.
Limerick Female,	Contract,	Repairing roofs of prison buildings; renewing laundry boiler, and whitewashing interior of laundry; painting and papering matron's dining room; painting and colouring walls of St. Clare's chapel and vestry; renewing heating furnace of bath entrance and of airing up furnace cell; forming two concrete steps for exercise in pump and ball yard, &c.; also in passage; building in recesses; fixing new gutters around prison buildings with down pipes; fixing and connecting with sewer gully traps water down pipes; forming new servants' sleeping room.
Do.,	Prison,	General repairing of gas, heating, and water pipes; repairing W.C. in ward, baths, and pump yards; painting, glazing, and whitewashing throughout the prison.

TABLE XXII.—WORKS OF RECONSTRUCTION, REPAIRS, &c.—continued.

Prisons.	Labour (Contract or Prison).	Detail of Works.
Londonderry,	Contract,	Re-constructing electric bell system; fitting up two new water closets, male prison; painting front of Governor's house depending windows and doors); repairing new room in Governor's house, and two rooms in matron's quarters, also keeping in repair warm, gutters, and down pipes, heating pipes, and gas and water pipes.
Do.	Prison,	Completing works in connection with enlargement and ventilation of 11 cells, male prison; attending with wood stone study pipes, male prison; erecting and fitting up new Protestant chapel; fixing in old lavatories steps to entrance in ward, and of drain pipes; stripping of chests, and cleaning ceiling of cook-house; laying 60 square yards of flagging in kitchen yard with another drain; fixing in stone new grates in officers' quarters; opening new door from matron's sitting room to bath room; fixing new floor in south at entrance to Protestant chapel, and plastering 80 feet of ceiling and walls leading to same; repairing windows, doors, furniture, yards, roads, and walls.
Mountjoy,	Contract,	Nil.
Do.	Prison,	Repairing roofs, and repairing and painting roof lights; repairing furniture, bedsteads, heating pipes, &c., in prison, baths, and cook-house; lowering pinnacle and re-setting coping at end of new wing; re-building parapet walls over infirmary wall damaged by masons; cleaning, whitening, and painting officers' quarters; repairing and cleaning roads, paths, &c.; cleaning and whitewashing cells and corridors of prison and offices, and painting woodwork and ironwork.
Sligo,	Contract,	Repairing roof of prison, and portions of Governor's house; painting and graining entrance and inside of two doors at entrance, and outside of Governor's hall door; repairing tank in laundry; repairing ceilings at front gate, and flooring three rooms; altering gas fittings to officers' sleeping rooms; fitting up flushing barrel at new cottages; painting boundary wall all round for 6 feet from top downwards; re-setting boiler in laundry, and fitting up new bath, water tank; removing and water cistern to heating apparatus lot; new cells in female prison to a higher position; altering of gas at front gate quarters; repairing cisterns and from prison to Governor's house.
Do.	Prison,	Replacing 8 iron doors in different parts of the prison by new wooden doors, fitted with locks, &c.; replacing of locks on iron doors by new ones; fixing new window frames and sashes in one wing and one officer's room; repairing dining room in chief warder's quarters; converting officers' room at top of corridors into stores, and female stairs, (2) into sleeping rooms for male officers, and supplying the latter with new floors; fixing up new door in entrance hall; re-moving iron chevaux-de-frise round boundary yards; fitting up spare room in female prison as private clothing store; general painting, whitewashing, and other repairs throughout the prison.
Tralee,	Contract,	Cleaning out 2 cess pits; repairing and painting sitting rooms of 2 warders' cottages; repairing bell at front gate, and electric bell; repairing hot water pipes in officers' mess and connecting tap to their landing; repairing supply pipe to heating boiler.
Do.	Prison,	Making and fitting up new stairs in main reception, and putting in new sheeting in reception; painting and colouring chief warder's office; whitening and painting chief warder's quarters and fitting up new window blinds; opening wall at back of hospital, repairing cesspits, and rebuilding wall; re-setting flagging at front of prison; repairing out stone paving steps between front gates; putting new sunk concrete coping for 70 yards of outer limit boundary wall of prison; pointing and whitewashing the entire prison; general repairs to roads, glazing, &c., repairs to locks and keys.
Tullamore,	Contract,	Repairing heating apparatus in female prison; repairing water supply of laundry; supplying pipes, &c., and fitting up gas connection in hospital and reception of female prison; repairing gas lamp; fixing lamp to female prison.

TABLE XXII.—WORKS OF RECONSTRUCTION, REPAIRS, &c.—*continued.*

Prison.	Labour (Convict or Prison).	Detail of Works.
Tullamore, .	Prison, .	Repairing doors in offices, mess, quarters, &c.; benefiting 4 cells in male prison; fixing 7 pairs of shutters in hospital, quarters, &c.; repairing windows and skylight in laundry; fixing 2 new doors and frames in female prison; repairing gas and water pipes; repairing tanks and gutters; repairing iron drains in main school; remodelling bridge connecting main prison with No. 4 block; including roofs and gutters; main school; whitewashing and painting prison; repairing 2 rooms in Quarters; hours; whitewashing and painting 4 cottages and papering 4 rooms.
Waterford, .	Contract,	Repairing heating chamber and hot-water pipes in washhouse; fitting up new bath-room in laundry; repairing... cistern; painting down new water supply to store yard for prisoners' use; repairing pump and putting new copper rod in same.
Do., .	Prison, .	Making and fitting up large library press for officers' and prisoners' books in male hall; erecting new coal house in store yard and pulling down concrete floor in the yard; repairing the defects in heating of 3 cells; roof of male and 3 cell of female prison; cleaning out the large water supply tank; top of prison and covering same with new boarding; repairing doors in male hall; altering and rebuilding W.C. in male exercise yard; painting, graining, and varnishing large entrance gate, and painting rails around front; general repairs to prison and cell furniture; painting, glazing, and whitewashing, &c., throughout the prison; repairing officers' quarters, hot mess-room, &c.
Wexford.	Contract,	Replastering 2 rooms in the prison hospital.
Do., .	Prison, .	Removing old house in chief warder's yard, and building up the descent leading to adjoining yard; making a new ashpit and frames for chief warder's quarters, and re-flashing the top rooms; glazing, painting, and whitewashing throughout the chief warder's quarters; remodelling floor of matron's kitchen, and re-flashing with hearth; putting up partition and new door and frame; painting, whitewashing, and repairing officers' quarters at front gate; general repairs throughout the prison, such as plumbing, painting, glazing, repairing furniture, &c.

MINOR PRISONS.

Carrick-on-Shannon,	Contract,	Taking down and removing ruined old kitchen in enlarged exercise yard attached to hospital; painting with cement 240 feet of coping on boundary wall in front of prison; also painting with cement 250 feet of coping on division walls in exercise yards; putting a small close coping ridge and one trestle over gate in warders' quarters; repairing sundry heads, &c., in connection with heating pipes.
Do., .	Prison, .	General whitewashing in prison, painting skirtings of walls, &c.
Drogheda, .	Contract,	Removing and painting 6 skylights on top of main prison and putting in 12 panes of ribbed glass in same; renewing hops of chimney and joints of brick of north wall; supplying new ball-cock to female prison W.C.; repairing large gates; new hinge to gate at front store.
Do., .	Prison, .	General limewashing of prison and walls of yards; painting of iron and wood work of prison doors, gates, &c.
Enniskillen, .	Contract,	Repairing roof of female prison after storm; removing old glass door and putting up new one; excavating ground for new sewer and laying earthenware sewerage pipes from chief warder's quarters, male and female prisons; also 3 inspection pits and heading back in connection with same; repairing water pipes in male prison and scullery of chief warder's quarters; putting up new panes, and repairs to broken plaster on gate lodge; putting new lock on office door.

TABLE XXII.—WORKS OF RECONSTRUCTION, REPAIRS, &c.—*continued.*

Minor Prisons.	Labour (Contract or Prison)	Detail of Works.
Enniskillen, .	Prison,	General whitewashing, painting, and glazing throughout the prison.
Mullingar, .	Contract,	Repairing kitchen range and supplying new fire cover; renewing ceiling over staircase of gate quarters; reslating roof of gate quarters with new lead, and replastering ceilings with cement; making two new fine grates at gate quarters; repairing W.C. at office; repairing 2 water-pumps; repairing and cleaning 2 office-stoves.
Do., .	Prison,	Limewashing walls and ceilings of cells and corridors of stores, officers' quarters and yards attached, and of six W.C.'s; cleaning and varnishing chapel and yard doors, and entrance gate and door; painting windows, cell doors, and skirtings, and yard gates; glazing windows; cleaning prison walks, and repairing prison implements.
Omagh,	Contract,	Repairing water-taps to female prisoners' bath, and exercise yard; repairing lead water-pipe and gully in chief warder's quarters; supplying new grate to bedroom, and fitting up sink and in warder's quarters; repairing flue pipe of stove for scalding prisoners' food; cleaning supply pipe to boardroom W.C., and repairing lead cistern.
Do., .	Prison,	New roof repairs to roofs of prison, chapel, and cookshed, and putting on 40 feet of new eave-gutters; painting and pebble-dashing part of outer walls; repairing W.C. in chief warder's quarters; putting new locks on presses to stores; putting up new lamp-post in front of prison; painting prison and general repairs to woodwork, plastering, glazing, &c., and limewashing cells and corridors, and painting woodwork and ironwork.
Wicklow, .	Contract,	Repairing force-pump and fixing new casing; fitting new grate in chief warder's office and one in gate warder's quarters; fixing new R.F. cock in gate warder's quarters; repairing W.C. in hall; repairing heating pipes.
Do., .	Prison,	General limewashing of prison, walls, yards, closets, &c.; painting iron and wood-work of gates, doors, &c.; throughout the prison.

BRIDEWELLS.

Ballishannon, .	Contract,	Resetting range in keeper's quarters; setting new grate, papering bedroom, and repairing ceiling of same.
Ballina, .	Contract,	Repairing crack in wall of exercise yard; painting coping on bridewell wall.
Boalry, .	Contract,	Repairing roof and chimney of bridewell.
Clifden, .	Contract,	New store kitchen range; renewing old planks, number, grate, &c., bottom of oven walls, and putting on coping of doorstep; renewing jambs of entrance door and rough-casting walls around same.
Kilrush, .	Contract,	Cleaning out cesspit, cleaning 4 chimneys, repairing door of female prison, whitewashing front and one end of bridewell; repairing paving.
Longford, .	Contract,	Limewashing tower rooms.
Newry, .	Contract,	Plastering, sizing, and papering walls of keeper's office and sizing rising; fitting up 20 gallon boiler in cookhouse; repairing defective slates on roof; puttying with cement framework of 3 windows in keeper's quarters.
New Ross, .	Contract,	Repairing roof.
Youghal, .	Contract,	Introducing water supply from town and repairing chimney of bridewell.

TABLE XXII.—WORKS OF RECONSTRUCTION, REPAIRS, &c.—*continued.*
LOCK-UP.

Name of Prison.	Labour (Convict or Prison.)	Detail of Work.
Ennis . . .	Prison, .	Pointing hall door and staircase of chief warder's quarters, whitewashing two rooms of same.

CONVICT PRISONS

Grangegorman,	Criminal,	Repairing the sluicing, pointing, filling, and replastering of roof, repairing coating of chimneys.
Do., .	Prison, .	Carrying out the necessary repairs in carpentry, plumbing, gasfitting, bellhanging, and glazing.
Maryborough,	Criminal,	Regulating and cleaning the prison turret clock.
Do., .	Prison, .	Fixing two new boilers and repairing three boilers in prisoners' cookhouse, fitting up a new boiler in C. prison; lifting tile front porches and woodwork of two warders' cottages, also new pavement and floor of prisoners' cookhouse; carpentry; fixing up a new water trough in surgery; replacing two sink traps in A and B yard, and fixing two new sinks in warders' cottages; repairing and pointing doctor's house; repairing the hot air heating; pointing hall, doors, staircases and corridors of prison, whitewashing cells and inside walls of prison and warders' quarters, making a mortar house; extending shed of A and B yard 12 feet, and relaying same with corrugated iron; slating the foundation and building with concrete a wall outside prison farm 132 yards long, the average height, including foundation, being 13 feet; also a further length of same wall 70 yards long and 5 feet in height, and so far off out of same making the foundation 175 yards in length and filling same with concrete to the depth of two feet 6 inches; building a weighbridge and erecting a weighbridge on prison farm; slating the first floor farm to railway 600 yards in length, depth varying from 4 inches to 4 feet.
Mountjoy, Do., .	Convict Prison, .	Nil. Continuing and completing 25 warders' cottages; building yard and boundary walls; forming roadways and footways, and hanging between gates; putting down 755 yards of concrete paths in exercise rings, and repairing, relaying, and pointing in cement 172 yards of granite paths; cleaning, whitening, painting, and papering 20 warders' cottages; cleaning, whitening, painting, and papering all of warder's quarters; putting down new floors and flooring in one room of Deputy Governor's house, and fitting up flushing tank for W.C., &c., and making 3 new sash cord mortells and grates in basement warders' quarters; making 1 new pair of gates for forge yard, with hinges, bolts, &c., and rebuilding part of piers; fitting and fixing with new frames of ovens in bakery; remaking oven cart and repairing Kitchen; making for Armagh prison 6 pairs of trestles and frames, 4 doors and frames, 1 staircase, and 1 closet seat; making for Grangegorman prison 1 bookcase, 14 picture frames, and 2 four-fold screens; making for Maryborough prison 1 pair of large gates, with hinges, bolts, &c., 2 large tubs for washing meat, 6 wheelbarrows, 12 handbarrows, and 1 cart; making for Kilmainham prison 16 pairs of trestles and frames, 4 doors and frames, and 1 staircase, 4 wheelbarrows, 25 mortar hods, and 12 cell stools; making for Limerick male prison 14 picture frames, 1 bookcase, 1 table, 6 wheelbarrows, 16 wooden beds, and 10 cell stools; making for Cork male prison 1 table and 1 carrying chair; making 2 meat boxes for Cork female prison; making 4 washing boards for Kilkenny prison; making 6 closet seats for Tralee prison; making 1 wheelbarrow for Tullamore prison; making 5 anthropometric stands, repairing roofs and repairing and painting roof lights; repairing furnaces, boilers, heating pipes, &c., in the prison and hospital, and in the laundry, baths, cookhouse, &c.; general repairs to buildings, boundary walls, &c., including brick and stonework, ironwork, plumbing, gasfitting, locks, gates, &c.; whitewashing the walls of cells, corridors, &c., and painting woodwork and ironwork.

TABLE XXIII.—RETURNS SHOWING EMPLOYMENT OF PRISONERS IN LOCAL AND CONVICT PRISONS AND ESTIMATED VALUE OF THEIR EARNINGS.

(As required by 40-41 Vict., cap. 49, section 16).

(A.) *Return showing the Prisons in which each Description of Employment has been carried on during the Year.*

Description of Employment.	Prisons in which carried on.	Total Number of Prisons.
I.—Non-productive . . .	—	NO.
II.—In Manufactures:—		
Bootmaking, ...	Mountjoy Local, ...	1
Knitting and needleworking,	Belfast, Castlebar, Cork F., Grangegorman Local, Limerick F., Londonderry, Sligo, Tullamore, Wexford, Drogheda, Grangegorman Convict.	11
Making Mail bags, . .	Kilmainham, ...	1
Matmaking, plaiting, and other work connected therewith.	Belfast, Cork M., Dundalk, Galway, Kilkenny, Limerick M., Londonderry, Mountjoy Local, Sligo, Wexford, Mountjoy Convict.	11
Picking or teasing oakum, hair, &c.	All prisons except Cork F., Limerick F., Maryborough and Grangegorman Convict.	34
Sackmaking, ...	Kilmainham, Mountjoy Local, Tullamore,	3
Shoemaking, ...	Armagh, Belfast, Kilkenny, Kilmainham, Limerick M., Londonderry, Mountjoy Local, Wexford, Maryborough, Mountjoy Convict.	10
Smithing, ...	Armagh, Belfast, Cork M., Limerick M., Londonderry, Tullamore, Waterford.	7
Stonebreaking, . . .	Armagh, Belfast, Castlebar, Clonmel, Cork M., Dundalk, Galway, Kilkenny, Kilmainham, Limerick M., Londonderry, Mountjoy Local, Sligo, Tralee, Tullamore, Waterford, Wexford, Drogheda, Enniskillen, Mullingar, Omagh.	21
Tailoring, ...	Armagh, Belfast, Kilkenny, Londonderry, Mountjoy Local, Tralee, Maryborough, Mountjoy Convict.	8
Washing, not including prisoners' clothing.	Armagh, Belfast, Castlebar, Clonmel, Cork F., Galway, Grangegorman Local, Limerick F., Londonderry, Sligo, Tralee, Tullamore, Waterford, Wexford.	14
Woodcutting. .	Armagh, Belfast, Clonmel, Cork M., Dundalk, Galway, Kilkenny, Kilmainham, Limerick M., Londonderry, Mountjoy Local, Sligo, Tralee, Tullamore, Waterford, Wexford, Drogheda, Enniskillen, Mullingar, Omagh, Mountjoy Convict.	21
Carpet cleaning, . .	Londonderry, ...	1
Linen cutting, . . .	Belfast, ...	1
Waving, ...	Mountjoy Local, ...	1
Tinsmithing, . . .	Kilkenny, Limerick Male, Mountjoy Local, Waterford, Mountjoy Convict.	5
Carpentry, . . .	Limerick M., Tralee, Waterford, Mountjoy Convict.	4

(A.)—continued—Return showing the Prisons in which each **Description** *of Employment has been carried on during the Year.*

Description of Employment.	Prisons in which carried on.	Total Number of Prisons.
III.—In Buildings:—		
Bricklayers or masons,	Armagh, Belfast, Clonmel, Cork M., Galway, Kilkenny, Kilmainham, Limerick M., Londonderry, Tralee, Mountjoy Convict.	11
Carpenters or joiners,	Armagh, Belfast, Clonmel, Cork M., Dundalk, Galway, Kilkenny, Kilmainham, Limerick M., Londonderry, Sligo, Tralee, Tullamore, Mullingar, Omagh, Maryborough, Mountjoy Convict.	17
Labourers,	All prisons except Castlebar, Clonmel, Cork F., Limerick M., Limerick F., Sligo, Wexford, Carrick, Drogheda, Enniskillen, Wicklow, and Grangegorman Convict.	17
Painters and glaziers,	All prisons except Cork F., Grangegorman Convict, Maryborough, and Grangegorman Convict.	11
Plasterers,	Belfast, Kilmainham, Omagh, Mountjoy Convict.	4
Plumbers and gasfitters,	Belfast.	1
Smiths,	Belfast, Clonmel, Cork M., Galway, Londonderry, Sligo, Omagh, Maryborough, Mountjoy Convict.	9
Whitewashers,	All prisons except Maryborough and Grangegorman Convict.	21
Stonebreaking for macadamising, &c.	Mountjoy Local.	1
Stonecutters,	Cork M.	1
IV.—In the ordinary service of the Prison:—		
Cleaning and jobbing work in and about the rooms, &c.	All prisons,	23
Cooking for the prisoners,	All prisons except Grangegorman Local, Carrick, Enniskillen, Mullingar, Omagh, Wicklow.	18
Labourers.	Enniskillen and Maryborough.	2
Nursing and attending sick prisoners, children, &c.	Armagh, Belfast, Clonmel, Cork M., Cork F., Galway, Kilmainham, Limerick M., Limerick F., Londonderry, Mountjoy Local, Sligo, Tralee, Tullamore, Waterford, Drogheda, Omagh.	17
Pumping water for the prison.	Castlebar, Clonmel, Cork M., Dundalk, Kilkenny, Kilmainham, Limerick M., Waterford, Wexford, Mullingar, Wicklow.	11
Repairing all kinds of prison clothing.	All prisons except Mountjoy Convict and Grangegorman Convict.	27
Repairing all kinds of prison shoes.	Armagh, Belfast, Castlebar, Clonmel, Cork M., Dundalk, Galway, Kilkenny, Kilmainham, Limerick M., Londonderry, Mountjoy Local, Sligo, Tralee, Tullamore, and Wexford.	16
Repairing all kinds of prison utensils.	Armagh, Belfast, Clonmel, Cork M., Galway, Limerick M., and Sligo.	7
Repairing and binding books,	Cork M., Mountjoy Convict.	2
Stoking prison furnaces,	Belfast, Clonmel, Kilkenny, Kilmainham, Limerick M., Londonderry, Tullamore, Waterford, Mountjoy Convict.	9
Upholsterers,	Kilmainham.	1
Washing prisoners' clothing.	All prisons except Limerick M., Mountjoy Local, and Grangegorman Convict.	24
Woodcutting.	Kilmainham, Wicklow.	2
Gardening.	Armagh, Belfast, Cork M., Dundalk, Galway, Kilkenny, Londonderry, Sligo, Tralee, Drogheda, Enniskillen, and Maryborough.	12
Baking for prisoners,	Cork M., Mountjoy Convict.	2

(B.)—*Separate Returns from each Prison.*

ARMAGH PRISON.

Returns by the Governor, showing the employment of the Prisoners and value of their Earnings during the year ended 31st March, 1897.

Description of Employment.	Daily Average Number of Prisoners (for working days of the year).			Value of Prisoners' Labour.			Total.
	M.	F.	Total.	£	s.	d.	£ s. d.
In Manufactures:—							
Picking or teasing oakum, hair, &c.	18·66	1·56	20·12	22	16	7	
Shoemaking.	·21	—	·21	3	1	7	
Smithing.	·02	—	·02	0	12	5	
Stonebreaking.	40·29	—	40·29	42	6	2	
Tailoring.	·04	4·	4·04	4	15	6	
Washing, not including prisoners' clothing.	—	1·	1·	7	2	1	
Woodcutting.	0·02	—	0·02	18	14	6	
Total	46·23	6·56	65·91				100 10 1
In Buildings:—							
Bricklayers or masons.	·12	—	·12	4	12	6	
Carpenters or joiners.	·21	—	·21	7	15	0	
Labourers.	·64	—	·60	16	23	4	
Painters and glaziers.	·03	—	·03	17	6	9	
Whitewashers.	·28	·06	·34	8	19	0	
Total	1·79	·06	1·85				44 16 4
In the ordinary service of the Prison:—							
Cleaning and jobbing work in and about the prison and prison yard and buildings (exclusive of building work of any kind).	4·61	1·72	6·48	103	2	8	
Cooking for the prisoners.	3·	—	5·	60	14	6	
Nursing and attending sick prisoners.	·03	1·71	1·74	31	1	0	
Repairing all kinds of prison clothing.	·11	10·79	10·91	100	6	0	
Repairing all kinds of prison shoes.	·74	—	·74	14	3	9	
Repairing all kinds of prison utensils.	·06	—	·06	6	17	6	
Washing prisoners' clothing.	—	4·02	4·02	66	11	0	
Gardening.	·22	—	·22	3	9	6	
Total	9·52	17·26	24·58				420 16 11
Non-effective:—							
Sick.	3·15	·66	1·81	—			
Under punishment.	·17	·09	·26	—			
Unemployed:—							
Awaiting trial.	2·	·72	2·02	—			
Debtors.	·09	—	·09	—			
First class misdemeanants.	·09	—	·09	—			
Others, &c.	1·56	·06	1·61	—			
Total	3·92	1·49	7·45	—			
Grand Total	23·42	25·90	62·77	—			666 3 4

BELFAST PRISON.

Return by the Governor, showing the employment of the Prisoners and value
of their Earnings during the year ended 31st March, 1897.

Description of Employment.	Daily Average Number of Prisoners (Per working days of the year).			Value of Prisoners' Labour.			Total.		
	M.	F.	Total.	£	s.	d.	£	s.	d.
In Manufacture:—									
Knitting and needleworking,	—	39·61	39·61	155	18	5			
Materialing, plaiting, and other work connected therewith,	77·32	—	77·32	109	17	9			
Picking or teazing oakum, hair, &c.,	58·31	7·84	78·13	139	8	9			
Shoemaking,	4·31	—	4·31	118	13	7			
Smithing,	1·90	—	1·90	37	17	9			
Stonebreaking,	78·71	—	78·71	204	5	16			
Tailoring,	5·90	—	5·90	138	11	3			
Washing, not including prisoners' clothing,	—	8·33	8·33	87	18	9			
Woodsawing,	1·32	—	1·32	3	4	1			
Linen cutting,	1·94	19·14	20·25	104	13	2			
Total,	147·98	69·98	216·98				1,147	0	10
In Buildings:—									
Bricklayers or masons,	·70	—	·70	20	18	3			
Carpenters or joiners,	1·32	—	1·32	27	11	4			
Labourers,	35·94	—	35·94	441	18	9			
Painters and glaziers,	1·71	—	1·71	34	4	9			
Plasterers,	·90	—	·90	7	13	8			
Plumbers and gasfitters,	·69	—	·69	18	18	0			
Smiths,	·87	—	·87	33	13	0			
Whitewashers,	·76	—	·76	2	16	3			
Total,	36·17	—	36·17				621	14	1
In the ordinary service of the Prison:—									
Cleaning and jobbing work in and about the prison and prison yard, and buildings (exclusive of building work of any kind),	9·31	4·90	14·31	295	19	5			
Cooking for the prisoners,	8·93	—	8·93	178	3	10			
Nursing and attending sick prisoners,	·91	·91	·99	0	6	1			
Repairing all kinds of prison bedding,	4·91	8·09	12·99	911	2	7			
Repairing all kinds of prison shoes,	4·19	—	8·10	64	13	5			
Repairing all kinds of prison utensils,	·91	—	·91	3	19	3			
Baking prison farinors,	·90	—	·90	13	18	1			
Washing prisoners' clothing,	—	2·93	8·93	178	13	9			
Gardening,	1·90	—	1·90	34	19	6			
Total,	27·95	17·73	45·95				940	7	1
Non-effectives:—									
Sick,	·99	·42	3·41	—					
Under punishment,	·99	·94	2·94	—					
Unemployed:—									
Awaiting trial,	20·31	3·09	23·31	—					
Debtors,	·71	·11	·11	—					
First class misdemeanants,	·90	·91	·91	—					
Others, &c.,	57·95	2·99	56·25	—					
Total,	86·69	12·11	83·92	—			3,394	2	0
Grand Total,	301·98	95·95	382·94	—			3,394	2	0

F

CASTLEBAR PRISON.

Return by the Governor, shewing the employment of the Prisoners and value of their Earnings during the year ended 31st March, 1867.

Description of Employment	Daily Average Number of Prisoners (on working days of the year)			Value of Prisoners' Labour	Total
	M.	F.	Total.	£ s. d.	£ s. d.
In Manufactures:—					
Knitting and woollen-weaving,	—	7·98	7·98	42 17 9	
Picking or Teasing hair, coir, &c.,	1·56	—	1·56	—	
Shoemaking,	11·48	—	11·48	2 15 7	
Washing, not including prisoners' clothing,	—	·99	·99	2 3 9	47 16 1
Total,	12·99	8·79	15·62		
In Buildings:—					
Painters and Glaziers,	·18	—	·18	3 3 8	
Whitewashers,	·29	—	·29	3 1 0	6 4 8
Total,	·29	—	·29		
In the ordinary service of the Prison:—					
Cleaning and holding work in and about the prison and prison yard and buildings (not paid or building work of any kind),	9·55	·21	9·66	114 15 3	
Cooking for the prisoners,	·—	—	·—	·94 19 7	
Pumping water for the service of the prison daily,	·99	—	·99	3 6 3	
Repairing all kinds of prison clothing,	·19	1·95	1·95	25 11 4	
Repairing all kinds of prison shoes,	·99	—	·99	5 6 4	
Washing prisoners' clothing,	—	1·90	1·90	34 16 4	214 12 4
Total,	9·99	3·90	13·62		
Non-effective:—					
Sick,	·95	·97	·96	—	
Under punishment,	·15	·49	·19	—	
Unemployed:—					
Awaiting trial,	·99	·91	·91	—	
First class misdemeanants,	·49	—	·99	—	
Others, &c.,	7·99	38	1·99	—	
Total,	9·99	·64	9·99		
Grand Total,	26·94	8·	1·99	—	268 13 8

CLONMEL (MALE) PRISON.

Return by the Governor, shewing the employment of the Prisoners and value of their Earnings during the year ended 31st March, 1867.

Description of Employment	Daily Average Number of Prisoners (on working days of the year)	Value of Prisoners' Labour	Total.
	M.	£ s. d.	£ s. d.
In Manufactures:—			
Picking or teasing oakum, hair, &c.,	11·9	4 17 11	
Shoemaking,	·96	7 14 4	
Washing, and including prisoners' clothing,	8·25	11 15 16	
Woodcutting,	6·97	99 5 9	
Total,	26·46		160 1 1

CLONMEL (MALE) PRISON—*continued.*

Return by the Governor, showing the employment of the Prisoners and value of their Earnings during the year ended 31st March, 1897.

Description of Employment	Daily Average Number of Prisoners (for working days of the year).	Value of Prisoners' Labour.	Total.
	No.	£ s. d.	£ s. d.
In Buildings :—			
Bricklayers or masons,			
Carpenters or joiners,			
Painters and glaziers,			
Smiths,			
Whitewashers,			
Total,			
In the ordinary service of the Prison :—			
Cleaning and rubbing work in and about the prison and prison yard and buildings (exclusive of building work of any kind),			
Cooking for the prisoners,			
Nursing and attending sick prisoners,			
Pumping water for the service of the prison only,			
Repairing all kinds of prison clothing,			
Repairing all kinds of prison shoes,			
Repairing all kinds of prison utensils,			
Picking prison oakum,			
Washing prisoners' clothing,			
Total,			
Non-effective :—			
Sick,			
Under punishment,			
Unemployed :—			
Awaiting trial,			
Debtors,			
First class misdemeanants,			
Others, &c.,			
Total,			
Grand Total,			

CORK (MALE) PRISON.

Return by the Governor, showing the employment of the Prisoners and value of their Earnings during the year ended 31st March, 1897.

Description of Employment	Daily Average Number of Prisoners (for working days of the year).	Value of Prisoners' Labour.	Total.
	No.	£ s. d.	£ s. d.
In Manufactures :—			
Mat-making, plaiting, and other work connected therewith,			
Picking or teasing oakum, hair, &c.,			
Knitting,			
Shoemaking,			
Woodcutting,			
Total,			

CORK (MALE) PRISON—*continued.*

Return by the Governor, showing the employment of the Prisoners and value of their Earnings during the year ended 31st March, 1897.

Description of Employment.	Daily Average Number of Prisoners (for working days of the year).	Value of Prisoners' Labour.	Total.
	M.	£ s. d.	£ s. d.
In Buildings :—			
Bricklayers or masons,	·04	12 0 6	
Carpenters or joiners,	·66	21 0 6	
Painters and glaziers,	·36	9 14 1	
Whitewashers,	·73	14 6 5	
Stonecutters,	·11	19 14 3	
Total,	2·54		85 16 0
In the ordinary service of the Prison :—			
Cleaning and jobbing work in and about the prison and prison yard and buildings (exclusive of building work of any kind),	24·34	442 0 9	
Cooking for the prisoners,	4·5	49 1 6	
Nursing and attending sick prisoners,	·55	5 0 0	
Pumping water for the service of the prison only,	4·09	111 9 9	
Repairing all kinds of prison clothing,	2·90	64 13 0	
Repairing all kinds of prison shoes,	1·96	25 2 0	
Repairing all kinds of prison utensils,	·69	1 14 3	
Repairing books,	·14	2 17 8	
Washing prisoners' clothing,	9·09	46 3 9	
Baking for prisoners,	2·6	23 5 0	
Total,	50·75		765 16 6
Non-effective :—			
Sick,	2·27	—	
Under punishment,	1·43	—	
Unemployed :—			
Awaiting trial,	3·59	—	
Debtors,	·70	—	
First class misdemeanants,	·66	—	
Others, &c.,	7·53	—	
Total,	16·08	—	
Grand Total,	134·37	—	1,013 10 13

CORK (FEMALE) PRISON.

Return by the Chief Wardress, showing the employment of the Prisoners and value of their Earnings during the year ended 31st March, 1897.

Description of Employment.	Daily Average Number of Prisoners (for working days of the year).	Value of Prisoners' Labour.	Total.
	F.	£ s. d.	£ s. d.
In Manufacture :—			
Knitting and needlework,	30·20	175 0 10	
Washing, not including prisoners' clothing,	1·40	9 13 3	
Total,	31·60		785 0 0
Buildings :—			
In Whitewashers,	·28	0 13 3	
Total,	·78		5 13 3

CORK (FEMALE) PRISON—continued.

Return by the Chief Warder, showing the employment of the Prisoners and value of their Earnings during the year ended 31st March, 1897.

Description of Employment.	Daily Average Number of Prisoners (the working days of the year).	Value of Prisoners' Labour.	Total.
	n.	£ s. d.	£ s. d.
In the ordinary service of the Prison:—			
Cleaning and jobbing work in and about the prison and prison yard and buildings (exclusive of building work of any kind),	9	181 16 0	
Cooking for the prisoners,	1	27 4 3	
Nursing prisoners' children,	3·93	—	
Repairing all kinds of prison clothing,	2 26	41 13 4	
Washing prisoners' clothing,	6·80	60 5 11	
Gardening,	2·0	2 5 3	
Total,	18		299 19 6
Non-effective:—			
Sick,	1	—	
Under punishment,	·95	—	
Unemployed:—			
Awaiting trial,	4	—	
Others, &c.,	3·33	—	
Total,	10·43	—	
Grand Total,	28	—	1,017 13 8

DUNDALK (MALE) PRISON.

Return by the Governor, showing the employment of the Prisoners and value of their Earnings during the year ended 31st March, 1897.

Description of Employment.	Daily Average Number of Prisoners (the working days of the year.)	Value of Prisoners' Labour.	Total.
	n.	£ s. d.	£ s. d.
In Manufactures:—			
Matmaking, plaiting, and other work connected therewith,	19·74	33 0 8	
Fishing or making cotton, hair, &c.,	9·46	2 5 2	
Stonebreaking,	9·64	3 9 5	
Woodmaking,	1·94	10 16 2	
Total,	32·74		48 11 3
In Buildings:—			
Carpenters or joiners,	·72	6 3 7	
Labourers,	4·8	82 14 4	
Painters and glaziers,	·63	13 13 1	
Whitewashers,	·28	4 8 0	
Total,	8·8		117 18 7
In the ordinary service of the Prison:—			
Cleaning and jobbing work in and about the prison and prison yard and buildings (exclusive of building work of any kind),	4·25	141 16 1	
Cooking for the prisoners,	1·54	47 7 4	
Pumping water for the service of the prison only,	2·95	95 14 0	
Repairing all kinds of prison clothing, &c.,	7·45	27 1 7	
Repairing all kinds of prison shoes,	·81	13 0 9	
Washing prisoners' clothing,	2·95	60 4 8	
Gardening,	3·2	60 12 0	
Total,	18·17		344 16 8

DUNDALK (MALE) PRISON—*continued.*

Return by the Governor, showing the employment of the Prisoners and value of their Earnings during the year ended 31st March, 1897.

Description of Employment.	Daily Average Number of Prisoners (for working days of the year).	Value of Prisoners' Labour.	Total.
	No.	£ s. d.	£ s. d.
Non-effective:—			
Sick,	·33	—	
Under punishment,	·37	—	
Unemployed:—			
Awaiting trial,	2·02	—	
Debtors,	·34	—	
First class misdemeanants,	·58	—	
Others, &c.,	4·14	—	
Total,	7·50	—	
Grand Total,	62·41	—	410 0 4

GALWAY PRISON.

Return by the Governor, showing the employment of the Prisoners and value of their Earnings during the year ended 31st March, 1897.

Description of Employment.	Daily Average Number of Prisoners (for working days of the year).			Value of Prisoners' Labour.	Total.
	M.	F.	Total.	£ s. d.	£ s. d.
In Manufacture:—					
Mat-making, plaiting, and other work connected therewith,	4·94	—	4·94	7 14 3	
Picking or teasing oakum, hair, &c.,	8·72	—	8·72		
Shoemaking,	18·96	—	18·96	72 14 11	
Washing, not including prisoners' clothing,	—	1·9	1·9	1 18 10	
Wool-carding,	1·08	—	1·08	16 9 5	
Total,	33·30	1·9	35·20	105 13 4
In Buildings:—					
Bricklayers or masons,	·13	—	·13	8 18 0	
Carpenters or joiners,	·35	—	·35	11 15 0	
Labourers,	6·19	—	6·19	124 2 8	
Painters and glaziers,	·16	—	·16	0 3 0	
Smiths,	·03	—	·03	6 18 0	
Whitewashers,	·09	—	·09	0 1 4	
Total,	7·84	—	7·84	160 8 0
In the ordinary service of the Prison:—					
Cleaning and jobbing work in and about the prison and prison yard and buildings (exclusive of building work of any kind),	3·37	1·0	4·37	62 12 9	
Cooking for the prisoners,	2·0	—	2·0	40 12 9	
Nursing and attending sick prisoners,	—	1·72	1·72	35 0 2	
Repairing all kinds of prison clothing,	·03	7·87	7·90	161 12 2	
Repairing all kinds of prison shoes,	·43	—	·43	8 7 5	
Repairing all kinds of prison utensils,	·01	—	·01	0 6 9	
Washing prisoners' clothing,	—	1·29	1·29	21 10 0	
Gardening,	1·02	—	1·02	39 5 4	
Total,	6·84	12·35	19·20	437 15 5

GALWAY PRISON—*continued.*

Return by the Governor, shewing the employment of the Prisoners and value of their Earnings during the year ended 31st March, 1897.

Description of Employment.	Daily Average Number of Prisoners (for working days of the year).			Value of Prisoners' Labour.	Total.
	M.	F.	Total.	£ s. d.	£ s. d.
Non-effective:—					
Sick,	1·25	·30	1·41	—	
Under punishment,	·84	·44	·20	—	
Unemployed:—					
Awaiting trial,	4·98	·25	2·22	—	
First class misdemeanants,	·01	—	·01	—	
Others, &c.,	8·25	·50	6·12	—	
Total,	9·62	2·48	11·14	—	
Grand Total,	58·12	13·38	72·46	—	647 10 7

GRANGEGORMAN (FEMALE) PRISON.

Return by the Superintendent, showing the employment of the Prisoners and value of their Earnings during the year ended 31st March, 1897.

Description of Employment.	Daily Average Number of Prisoners (for working days of the year).	Value of Prisoners' Labour.	Total.
	No.	£ s. d.	£ s. d.
In Manufactures:—			
Knitting and needlework,	104·?	1,575 13 2	
Washing, not including prisoners' clothing,	13·93	420 19 11	1,028 0 11
Total,	197·98		
In Buildings:—			
Labourers,	3·78	47 17 ?	
Whitewashers,	3·?	13 13 0	44 10 3
Total,	3·78		
In the ordinary service of the Prison:—			
Cleaning and kitchen work in and about the prison and prison yard and buildings (exclusive of building work of any kind),	13·87	332 18 2	
Repairing all kinds of prison clothing,	14	205 9 6	
Washing prisoners' clothing,	1·?	138 7 8	741 1 5
Total,	30·49		
Non-effective:—			
Sick,	7·94	—	
Under punishment,	·74	—	
Unemployed:—			
Awaiting trial,	19·47	—	
Others, &c.,	8·24	—	
Total,	19·98	—	
Grand Total,	293·?9	—	3,802 4 4

KILKENNY (MALE) PRISON.

Return by the Governor, showing the employment of the Prisoners and
value of their Earnings during the year ended 31st March, 1897.

Description of Employment.	Daily Average Number of Prisoners (five working days of the year).	Value of Prisoners' Labour.	Total.
	No.	£ s. d.	£ s. d.
In Manufactures :—			
Matmaking, platting, and other work connected therewith,	·80	13 5 0	
Picking or teasing oakum, hair, &c.,	14·04	3 13 9	
Shoemaking,	3·17	212 1 6	
Smithing, &c.,	·06	1 5 7	
Stonebreaking,	1·04	0 16 4	
Tailoring,	·45	12 0 11	
Woodcutting,	6·42	10 17 9	
Total,	27·31		199 13 1
In Buildings :—			
Bricklaying or masons,	·91	0 0 1	
Carpenters or joiners,	·40	19 16 8	
Labourers,	·45	4 13 4	
Painters and plasters,	·93	4 22 2	
Whitewashers,	·48	2 14 9	
Total,	3·35		31 4 3
In the ordinary service of the Prison :—			
Cleaning and jobbing work in and about the prison and kitchen yard and buildings (or classes of building work of any kind),	4·15	123 4 8	
Cooking for the prisoners,	2·22	58 9 11	
Pumping water for the service of the prison only,	6·15	·05 0 4	
Repairing all kinds of prison clothing,	3·54	48 10 4	
Repairing all kinds of prison shoes,	9·	37 15 4	
Stoking prison furnaces,	·40	·10 7 6	
Washing prisoners' clothing,	2·78	40 1 7	
Gardening,	·40	11 2 3	
Total,	29·25		427 6 9
Non-effective :—			
Sick,	·37	—	
Under punishment,	·74	—	
Unemployed :—			
Awaiting trial,	6·40	—	
First class misdemeanants,	·84	—	
Others, &c.,	8·06	—	
Total	12·04	—	
Grand Total,	75·10	—	658 2 6

KILMAINHAM (MALE) PRISON.

Return by the Governor, showing the employment of the Prisoners and
value of their Earnings during the year ended 31st March, 1891.

Description of Employment.	Daily average Number of Prisoners (the working days of the year).	Value of Prisoners' Labour.	Total.
	No.	£ s. d.	£ s. d.
In Manufactures:—			
Picking or teasing oakum, hair, &c.	10·75	2 5 6	
Tailoring,	1·36	4 7 1	
Shoemaking,	1·43	67 16 9	
Stonebreaking,	69·3	41 7 7	
Woodcutting,	7·11	23 18 4	
Making Mail bags,	3·75	59 8 7	
Total,	95·4		248 16 10
In Buildings:—			
Bricklayers or masons,	·9	33 7 2	
Carpenters or joiners,	1·	37 16 2	
Labourers,	9·4	133 17 5	
Painters and glaziers,	2·	65 18 9	
Plasterers,	·26	9 16 11	
Whitewashers,	1·	20 8 8	
Total,	13·82		361 12 4
In the ordinary service of the Prison:—			
Cleaning and jobbing work in and about the prison and prison yards and buildings (exclusive of building work of any kind),	1·22	118 0 11	
Cooking for the prisoners,	3·	104 18 0	
Nursing and attending sick prisoners,	·97	15 15 1	
Pumping water for the service of the prison only,	·5	36 18 7	
Repairing all kinds of prison clothing,	1·94	25 11 4	
Repairing all kinds of prison stock,	·07	90 8 2	
Stoking prison furnaces,	·5	30 18 9	
Washing prisoners' clothing,	1·	64 19 9	
Woodcutting,	2·	13 8 8	
Upholstering,	·15	7 3 11	
Labourers,	4·2	101 18 0	
Total,	94·62		741 17 7
Non-effective:—			
Sick,	4·73	—	
Under punishment,	·67	—	
Unemployed:—			
Awaiting trial,	33·13	—	
Debtors,	·41	—	
First class misdemeanants,	1·72	—	
Others, &c.,	13	—	
Total,	49·75	—	
Grand Total,	193·08	—	1,352 18 5

LIMERICK (MALE) PRISON,

Return by the Governor, showing the employment of the Prisoners and value of their Earnings during the year ended 31st March, 1897.

Descriptions of Employment.	Daily Average Number of Prisoners (per working days of the year.)	Value of Prisoners' Labour.	Total.
	No.	£ s. d.	£ s. d.
In Manufactures :—			
Mat-making, plaiting, and other work connected therewith,	24·15	10 15 11	
Tinning or tending colours, knit, &c.,	1·93	3 4 4	
Shoemaking,	—	0 2 4	
Smithing and cabinetry,	—	0 0 5	
Stonebreaking,	10·73	70 15 10	
Woodcutting,	3·23	33 18 11	
Tailormaking,	·22	3 8 3	137 3 0
Total,	41·14		
In Buildings :—			
Bricklayers or masons,	·87	18 10 2	
Carpenters or joiners,	·45	14 17 8	
Painters and glaziers,	·12	0 11 0	
Whitewashers,	·16	0 1 5	
Total,	1·48		44 3 0
In the ordinary service of the Prison :—			
Cleaning and jobbing work in and about the prison and prison yard and buildings (exclusive of building work of any kind),	2·41	141 18 7	
Cooking for the prisoners,	9·	94 5 0	
Nursing and attending sick prisoners,	·14	4 2 0	
Punishing water for cleansing of the prison only,	1·	8 11 0	
Repairing work for diminution of prison clothing,	1·31	33 9 10	
Repairing all kinds of prisoners' shoes,	·61	37 9 10	
Repairing all kinds of prison utensils,	·69	14 9 7	
Stoking prison furnaces,	·28	7 8 10	
Total,	14·13		373 4 0
Non-effective :—			
Sick,	2·61	—	
Under punishment,	·97	—	
Unemployed :—			
Awaiting trial,	4·08	—	
Debtors,	·94	—	
First-class misdemeanants,	·01	—	
Others, &c.,	0·95	—	
Total,	16·33	—	
Grand Total,	84·77	—	554 0 0

LIMERICK (FEMALE) PRISON.

Return by the Chief Warder, showing the employment of the Prisoners and value of their Earnings during the year ended 31st March, 1897.

Description of Employment.	Daily Average Number of Prisoners (for working days of the year.)	Value of Prisoners' Labour.	Total.
	v.	£. s. d.	£ s. d.
In Manufactures:—			
Knitting and needleworking,	·27	1 3 4	
Washing, not including prisoners' clothing,	1·00	1 5 6	
Total,	1·27		2 11 10
In Buildings:—			
Painters and glaziers,	·61	0 0 5	
Whitewashers,	·19	4 13 11	
Total,	·80		4 9 4
In the ordinary service of the Prison:—			
Cleaning and jobbing work in and about the prison, incl. prison yard, and buildings (exclusive of building work of any kind),	4·60	25 4 4	
Cooking for the prisoners,	1·68	9 12 7	
Nursing children,	·77	—	
Repairing all kinds of prison clothing,	11·74	20 14 3	
Washing prisoners' clothing,	1·16	0 3 3	
Total,	20·01		11 0 10
Non-effectives:—			
Sick,	1·82	—	
Under punishment,	·10	—	
Unemployed:—			
Awaiting trial, &c.,	1·04	—	
Penal class misdemeanants,	1·95	—	
Others, &c.,	5·15	—	
Total,	10·14	—	
Grand Total,	40·83	—	£27 13 1

LONDONDERRY PRISON.

Return by the Governor, showing the employment of the Prisoners and value of their Earnings during the year ended 31st March, 1897.

Description of Employment.	Daily Average Number of Prisoners (for working days of the year.)			Value of Prisoners' Labour.	Total.
	m.	f.	Total.	£ s. d.	£ s. d.
In Manufactures:—					
Knitting and woollenworking,	—	1·04	1·04	6 17 9	
Matmaking, Plaiting and other work connected therewith,	14·37	—	14·37	33 16 0	
Picking or teasing oakum, hair, &c.,	14·62	—	14·62	13 16 7	
Shoemaking,	·15	—	·15	2 15 0	
Smithing,	·74	—	·74	1 11 10	
Stonebreaking,	·77	—	·77	4 2 3	
Tailoring,	·99	—	·99	1 10 7	
Washing, not including prisoners' clothing,	—	·90	·90	4 1 10	
Woodcutting,	1·73	—	1·73	44 18 11	
Carpet cleaning,	·38	—	·38	16 16 11	
Total,	43·48	4·94	48·7		116 5 0

LONDONDERRY PRISON—*continued.*

Return by the Governor, showing the employment of the Prisoners and value
of their Earnings during the year ended 31st March, 1891.

Description of Employment.	Daily Average Number of Prisoners (for working days of the year.)			Value of Prisoners' Labour.			Total.		
	M.	F.	Total.	£	s.	d.	£	s.	d.
In Buildings :—									
Bricklayers or masons,	·33	—	·33	2	18	7			
Carpenters or joiners,	·08	—	·08	13	9	0			
Labourers, .	2·55	—	2·55	52	6	5			
Painters and glaziers,	·06	—	·06	15	11	10			
Smiths,	·21	—	·21	8	0	0			
Whitewashers, .	·57	—	·57	5	16	7			
Total, .	4·51		4·51				84	15	5
In the ordinary service of the Prison :—									
Cleaning and jobbing work in and about the prison and prison yard, and building (exclusive of building work of any kind),	8·73	1·75	10·48	110	1	7			
Cooking for the prisoners, .	—	2·	2·	60	10	2			
Nursing and attending sick prisoners,	1·25	·37	2·33	41	11	11			
Repairing all kinds of prison clothing,	1·	13·55	14·55	206	3	0			
Repairing all kinds of prison shoes,	·40	—	·40	13	6	0			
Stoking prison furnaces,	·37	—	·37	8	19	1			
Washing prisoners' clothing, . .	—	4·63	4·63	53	18	11			
Gardening, . . .	·02	—	·02	11	4	0			
Total, . . .	14·90	22·64	37·1				548	15	1
Non-effective :—									
Sick,	3·04	·98	3·72	—					
Under punishment, . . .	·38	·54	·92	—					
Unemployed :—									
Awaiting trial, . .	5·0	·07	6·78	—					
Debtors,	·4	·08	·42	—					
First class misdemeanants, . .	·50	·08	·52	—					
Others, &c., . . .	6·5	1·08	6·18	—					
Total, . . .	12·90	3·56	18·51	—					
Grand Total, . . .	34·81	25·14	65·95				799	18	9

MOUNTJOY (MALE) PRISON.

Return by the Governor, showing the employment of the Prisoners and value
of their Earnings during the year ended 31st March, 1897.

Description of Employment.	Daily Average Number of Prisoners (for working days of the year.)	Value of Prisoners' Labour.			Total.		
	N.	£	s.	d.	£	s.	d.
In Manufactures :—							
Brushmaking,	6·52	119	7	7			
Knitmaking, plaiting, and other work connected therewith,	21·68	57	2	10			
Picking or teasing oakum, hair, &c.,	11·62	28	5	5			
Sackmaking,	20·42	35	4	5			
Shoemaking,	8·95	147	2	8			
Smithing (do.),	·27	36	14	6			
Stonebreaking,	4·08	5	19	6			
Tailoring,	7·05	78	0	2			
Weaving linen, &c.,	8·10	117	4	6			
Woodcutting,	2·52	37	1	4			
Total,	217·97				444	9	1

MOUNTJOY (MALE) PRISON—*continued.*

Return by the Governor, showing the employment of the Prisoners and value of their Earnings during the year ended 31st March, 1897.

Description of Employment.	Daily Average Number of Prisoners (for working days of the year).	Value of Prisoners' Labour.	Total.
	M.	£ s. d.	£ s. d.
In Buildings:—			
Labourers,	8.94	310 11 8	
Painters and glaziers,	.89	19 4 2	
Stone-breaking,	30.56	160 0 8	
Whitewashers,	1.79	41 0 7	
Total,	37.19		573 16 0
In the ordinary service of the Prison :—			
Cleaning and jobbing work in and about the prison and prison yard and buildings (exclusive of building work of any kind),	14.43	273 5 4	
Cooking for the prisoners,	3.93	115 18 4	
Nursing and attending sick prisoners,	2.16	26 7 3	
Repairing all kinds of prison clothing,	4.58	85 14 6	
Repairing all kinds of prison shoes,	.94	10 5 2	
Total,	24.96		513 11 0
Non-Effective :—			
Sick,	12.71	—	
On the punishment,	.71	—	
Unemployed :—			
Debtors,	.02	—	
Others, &c.,	37.9	—	
Total,	49.99	—	
Grand Total,	329.66	—	1,591 0 8

SLIGO PRISON.

Return by the Governor, showing the employment of the Prisoners and value of their Earnings during the year ended 31st March, 1897.

Description of Employment.	Daily Average Number of Prisoners (for working days of the year).			Value of Prisoners' Labour.	Total.
	M.	F.	Total.	£ s. d.	£ s. d.
In Manufactories :—					
Knitting and needleworking,	—	4	4	0 13 4	
Matmaking, plaiting, and other work connected therewith,	3.96	—	3.96	4 14 6	
Picking or teasing oakum, hair, &c.,	8	—	8	1 14 0	
Stonebreaking,	12.08	—	12.08	14 0 0	
Washing, not including prisoners' clothing,	—	1	1	1 0 11	
Woodsplitting,	5.41	—	5.41	41 18 14	
Total,	29.46	5	34.46		64 11 0

SLIGO PRISON—*continued.*

Return by the Governor, showing the employment of the Prisoners and value of their Earnings during the year ended, 31st March, 1857.

Description of Employment.	Daily Average Number of Prisoners (for working days of the year).			Value of Prisoners' Labour.	Total.
	M.	F.	Total.	£ s. d.	
In Buildings:—					8 4 4
Carpenters or joiners,	·30	—	·30	2 2 2	
Painters and glaziers,	·13	—	·18	4 8 4	
Smiths,	·92	—	·92	2 16 6	
Whitewashers,	·19	—	·19	3 11 11	
Total,	·34		·34		17 15 9
In the ordinary service of the Prison:—					
Cleaning and keeping work in and about the prison and prison yard and buildings (exclusive of building work of any kind),	3·45	1·04	3·49	73 11 2	
Cooking for the prisoners,	1·	—	1·	20 4 6	
Nursing and attending sick prisoners,	·73	·08	·81	16 8 1	
Prison garden,	1·77	—	1·77	44 18 10	
Repairing all kinds of prison clothing,	·38	·91	1·29	39 17 9	
Repairing all kinds of prison shoes,	·96	—	·96	9 18 11	
Repairing all kinds of prison utensils,	·55	—	·55	9 11 8	
Washing prisoners' clothing,	—	2·24	2·26	48 15 11	
Total,	6·81	3·47	10·6		281 17 7
Non-effective:—					
Sick,	2·76	·17	2·89	—	
Under punishment,	·18	—	·18	—	
Unemployed:—					
Awaiting trial,	4·94	1·42	7·56	—	
Debtors,	·91	—	·91	—	
Exempt on payment for food,	·91	—	·91	—	
Others, &c.,	5·81	1·41	3·92	—	
Total,	11·87	3·91	16·00	—	
Grand Total,	43·66	3·18	82·68	—	333 4 9

TRALEE PRISON.

Return by the Governor, showing the employment of the Prisoners and value of their Earnings during the year ended 31st March, 1857.

Description of Employment.	Daily Average Number of Prisoners (for working days of the year).			Value of Prisoners' Labour.	Total.
	M.	F.	Total.	£ s. d.	
In Manufactures:—					6 4 4
Picking or teasing oakum, hair, &c.,	4·19	—	4·19	2 4 2	
Stonebreaking,	11·90	—	11·90	103 18 4	
Tailoring,	·99	—	·99	9 9 11	
Washing, not including prisoners' clothing,	·91	·19	·49	1 18 7	
Woodcutting,	2·	—	2·	5 19 8	
Total,	18·49	·19	18·30		114 7 7
In Buildings:—					
Bricklayers or masons,	·14	—	·14	4 1 3	
Carpenters or joiners,	·49	—	·49	10 16 9	
Labourers,	8·14	—	8·74	137 17 9	
Painters and glaziers,	·79	—	·79	23 4 6	
Whitewashers,	·94	—	·94	35 13 6	
Total,	11·04	—	11·04		167 13 6

TRALEE PRISON—continued.

RETURN by the Governor, showing the employment of the Prisoners and value of their Earnings during the year ended 31st March, 1897.

Description of Employment.	Daily Average Number of Prisoners (the working days of the year).			Value of Prisoners' Labour.	Total.
	M.	F.	Total.	£ s. d.	£ s. d.
In the ordinary service of the Prison :—					
Cleaning and jobbing work in and about the prison and prison yard, and buildings (exclusive of building work of any kind),	6·08	·71	7·14	5 0 0	
Cooking for the prisoners,	·01	1·19	1·20	11 9 5	
Gardening,	5	—	5	115 10 8	
Nursing and attending sick prisoners,	·61	·98	1·09	1 16 5	
Repairing all kinds of prison clothing,	·71	3·72	3·43	67 10 0	
Repairing all kinds of prison shoes,	·98	—	·98	2 6 8	
Washing prisoners' clothing,	—	·98	·98	16 4 8	
Total,	3·18	6·66	13·11		343 19 4
Non-effective :—					
Sick,	·44	—	·44	—	
Under punishment,	·21	·03	·22	—	
Unemployed :—					
Awaiting trial,	5·60	·95	5·65	—	
Debtors,	·01	·03	·04	—	
First class misdemeanants,	·03	1·1	·14	—	
Others, &c.,	1·11	·02	1·12	—	
Total,	7·14	·06	7·06	—	
Grand Total,	42·73	6·04	48·72	—	335 19 4

TULLAMORE PRISON.

RETURN by the Governor, showing the employment of the Prisoners and value of their Earnings during the year ended 31st March, 1897.

Description of Employment.	Daily Average Number of Prisoners (the working days of the year).			Value of Prisoners' Labour.	Total.
	M.	F.	Total.	£ s. d.	£ s. d.
In Manufactures :—					
Knitting and saddleworking,	—	1·97	1·97	1 4 5	
Picking or teasing oakum, hair, &c.,	11·88	—	11·88	—	
Shoemaking,	37·06	—	37·06	81 33 0	
Smithing,	·98	—	·98	6 7 21	
Stonebreaking,	1·3	—	1·3	—	
Washing, not including prisoners' clothing,	—	3·91	3·91	1 24 7	
Woodcutting,	·81	—	·81	0 5 11	
Total,	43·79	6·16	43·93		82 4 5
In Buildings :—					
Carpenters or joiners,	·56	—	·56	1 17 0	
Labourers,	1·93	—	1·93	54 3 4	
Painters and glaziers,	·93	—	·93	0 11 4	
Total,	1·92	—	1·93		55 6 5

TULLAMORE PRISON—*continued*.

Return by the Governor, showing the employment of the Prisoners and value of their Earnings during the year ended 31st March, 1897.

Description of Employment	Daily Average Number of Prisoners (the working days of the year).			Value of Prisoners' Labour.	Total.
	M.	F.	Total.	£ s. d.	£ s. d.
In the ordinary service of the Prison :—					
Cleaning and jobbing work in and about the prison and prison yard, and buildings (exclusive of building work of any kind),	4·11	·57	4·68	62 11 0	
Cooking for the prisoners,	2·	··	2·	36 2 4	
Knitting and attending sick prisoners,	·62	·16	·78	14 7 0	
Repairing all kinds of prison clothing,	·46	7·34	7·80	89 16 0	
Repairing all kinds of prison boots,	·47	—	·90	13 4 0	
Stoking picking furnaces,	·83	—	·36	13 2 0	
Washing prisoners' clothing,	·48	1·92	2·40	27 9 0	
Total,	9·12	9·34	19·27		707 9 9
Non-effective :—					
Sick,	1·00	2·10	3·11	—	
Under punishment,	·48	·62	·42	—	
Unemployed :—					
Awaiting trial,	6·01	·36	4·35	—	
Debtors,	·31	—	·34	—	
First class misdemeanants,	1·65	—	1·85	—	
Others, &c.,	6·12	1·96	7·79	—	
Total,	10·02	8·92	17·91	—	
Grand Total,	15·06	17·22	30·70	—	453 7 9

WATERFORD PRISON.

Return by the Governor, showing the employment of the Prisoners and value of their Earnings during the year ended 31st March, 1897.

Description of Employment.	Daily Average Number of Prisoners (the working days of the year).			Value of Prisoners' Labour.	Total.
	M.	F.	Total.	£ s. d.	£ s. d.
In Manufacture :—					
Knitting and needleworking,	—	2·46	2·46	1 4 4	
Picking or teasing oakum, hair, &c.,	3·59	—	2·49	1 5 0	
Building,	·41	—	·41	6 4 6	
Stonebreaking,	17·85	—	17·35	32 5 3	
Washing, not including prisoners' clothing,	—	4·73	4·73	66 15 3	
Woodcutting,	7·18	—	7·18	20 18 0	
Total,	27·43	7·19	34·62		158 8 6
In Buildings :—					
Labourers,	7·00	—	7·00	66 18 0	
Whitewashers,	·48	·13	·62	15 13 1	
Total,	2·50	·13	7·62		66 8 1

WATERFORD PRISON—*continued.*

Return by the Governor, showing the employment of the Prisoners and value of their Earnings during the year ended 31st March, 1897.

Description of Employment.	Daily average Number of Prisoners (for working days of the year.)			Value of Prisoners' Labour.	Total.
	M.	F.	Total.	£ s. d.	£ s. d.
In the ordinary service of the Prison :—					
Cleaning and jobbing work in and about the prison and prison yard and buildings (exclusive of building work of any kind),				115 15 5	
Cooking for the prisoners,	—			46 5 10	
Nursing and attending sick prisoners,				29 5 5	
Pumping water for the service of the prison only,		—		31 . 6	
Repairing all kinds of prison clothing,	—			247 18	
Stoking prison furnaces,		—		21 2 2	
Washing prisoners' clothing,	—			43 8 0	177 4 5
Total,					
Non-effective :—					
Sick,				—	
Under punishment,				—	
Unemployed :—					
Awaiting trial,				—	
Debtors,		—		—	
Except on payment for hard,				—	
Others, &c.,				—	
Total,				—	
Grand Total,				—	7 18 16 9

WEXFORD PRISON.

Return by the Governor, showing the employment of the Prisoners and value of their Earnings during the year ended 31st March, 1897.

Description of Employment.	Daily Average Number of Prisoners (for working days of the year.)			Value of Prisoners' Labour.	Total.
	M.	F.	Total.	£ s. d.	£ s. d.
In Manufactures :—					
Mat-making, plaiting, and other work connected therewith,		—		16 4 10	
Picking or teasing oakum, hair, &c.,				16 2 7	
Shoemaking,		—		0 1 0	
Stonebreaking,		—		2 9 0	
Washing, &c., (including prisoners' clothing)	—			0 16 10	
Woodcutting,				11 9 4	40 9 11
Total,					
In Buildings :—					
Painters and glaziers,				2 18 1	
Whitewashers,		—		1 16 4	4 9 5
Total,					

WEXFORD PRISON.—*continued.*

Return by the Governor, showing the employment of the Prisoners and value
of their Earnings during the year ended 31st March, 1897.

Description of Employment.	Daily Average Number of Prisoners (for working days of the year).			Value of Prisoners' Labour.	Total.
	M.	F.	Total.	£ s. d.	£ s. d.
In the ordinary service of the Prison:—					
Cleaning and painting work in and about the prison and prison yard, and buildings (exclusive of building work of any kind).	5·75	·64	6·39	36 4 3	
Cooking for the prisoners.	·49	·54	·63	30 0 0	
Pumping water for the service of the prison only.	·34	—	·34	13 13 3	
Repairing all kinds of prison clothing.	·49	1·93	2·41	52 6 6	
Repairing all kinds of prison shoes.	·31	—	·31	2 1 4	
Washing prisoners' clothing.	·40	·30	·70	13 3 4	
Total.	6·42	4·95	11·36		136 10 6
Non-effective:—					
Sick.	·34	·06	·38	—	
Under punishment.	·25	·03	·28	—	
Uninstructed:—					
Awaiting trial.	2·64	—	2·64	—	
Debtors.	·41	—	·11	—	
First class misdemeanants.	2·64	·24	1·93	—	
Others, &c.	1·44	·36	1·44	—	
Total.	4·14	·43	6·73	—	
Grand Total.	20·6	6·27	35·67		266 5 6

MINOR PRISONS.

CARRICK-ON-SHANNON PRISON.

Return by the Chief Warder, showing the employment of the Prisoners and
value of their Earnings during the year ended 31st March, 1897.

Description of Employment.	Daily Average Number of Prisoners (for working days of the year).			Value of Prisoners' Labour.	Total.
	M.	F.	Total.	£ s. d.	£ s. d.
In Manufactures:—					
Picking or teasing oakum, hair, &c.	·25	—	·25	—	
In Buildings:—					
Painters and glaziers.	·29	—	·29	0 18 3	
White-washers.	·16	—	·16	1 13 0	
Total.	·42	—	·42		2 19 3
In the ordinary service of the Prison:—					
Cleaning and painting work in and about the prison and prison yard, and buildings (exclusive of building work of any kind).	·59	·08	·67	1X 12 3	
Repairing all kinds of prison clothing.	—	·08	·08	1 1 0	
Washing prisoners' clothing.	—	·24	·24	2 16 3	
Total.	·14	·39	·47		15 3 6
Unemployed:—					
Awaiting trial.	1·74	·92	2·66	—	
Total.	1·74	·92	1·66	—	
Grand Total.	2·03	·91	2·94		22 1 6

DROGHEDA PRISON.

Return by the Chief Warder, showing the employment of the Prisoners and value of their Earnings during the year ended 31st March, 1897.

Description of Employment.	Daily Average Number of Prisoners (the working days of the year).			Value of Prisoners' Labour.	Total.
	M.	F.	Total.	£ s. d.	£ s. d.
In Manufacture:—					
Knitting and needleworking,	—	'09	'09	1 7 0	
Fishing nr making nets, bags, &c.,	'09	—	'09	0 3 0	
Stonebreaking,	'09	—	'09	0 3 0	
Woodcutting,	'10	—	'10	2 4 0	
Total,	'91	'09	1'25		4 5 0
In Buildings:—					
Painters and glaziers,	'09	—	'09	0 13 2	
Whitewashers,	'09	—	'09	2 3 3	
Total,	'10	—	'10		3 10 10
In the ordinary service of the Prison:—					
Cleaning and jobbing work in and about the prison and prison yard, and buildings (exclusive of building work of any kind),	'09	'09	'09	1f 13 9	
Cooking for the prisoners,	'09	'09	'09	10 15 5	
Nursing and attending children,	—	'09	'09	—	
Repairing all kinds of prison clothing,	'09	'09	'09	0 0 3	
Washing prisoners' clothing,	—	'09	'09	1 13 9	
Garden work,	'09	—	'09	0 3 9	
Total,	1'11	1'09	2'25		40 17 3
Non-effective:—					
Sick,	'09	'09	'09	—	
Under punishment,	—	'09	'09	—	
Unemployed:—					
Others, &c.,	1'77	'81	1'58	—	
Total,	1'58	'18	1'59	—	
Grand Total,	2'75	1'43	8'59	—	50 9 5

ENNISKILLEN PRISON.

Return by the Chief Warder, showing the employment of the Prisoners and value of their Earnings, during the year ended 31st March, 1897.

Description of Employment.	Daily Average Number of Prisoners (the working days of the year).			Value of Prisoners' Labour.	Total.
	M.	F.	Total.	£ s. d.	£ s. d.
Non-Remunerative,	'20	'09	'29	—	
In Manufacture:—					
Stonebreaking,	'07	—	'07	0 13 9	
Woodcutting,	'15	—	'15	0 17 2	
Total,	'28	—	'22		1 14 0
In Buildings:—					
Painters and glaziers,	'07	—	'07	1 17 4	
Whitewashers,	'21	'09	'09	2 17 14	
Total,	'28	'09	'09		7 4 14

ENNISKILLEN PRISON—*continued.*

Return by the Chief Warden, showing the employment of the Prisoners and value of their Earnings during the year ended 31st March, 1897.

Description of Employment.	Daily Average Number of Prisoners (for working days of the year).			Value of Prisoners' Labour.	Total.
	M.	*F.*	Total.	£ s. d.	£ s. d.
In the ordinary service of the Prison :— Cleaning and jobbing work in and about the prison and prison yard and buildings (exclusive of building work of any kind),	·22	·22	·47	0 13 1	
Gardening,	·06	—	·06	0 11 1	
Repairing all kinds of prison clothing,	·03	·09	·06	0 10 10	
Washing prisoners' clothing,	·08	·11	·19	1 11 5	14 0 7
Total,	·48	·33	·71		
Non-effective :—					
Sick,	·04	·04	·09	—	
Under punishment,	·01	—	·02	—	
Unemployed :—					
Awaiting trial,	·04	·12	·96	—	
Total,	·08	·16	1·06	—	
Grand Total,	1·08	·48	1·78	—	16 1 2

MULLINGAR PRISON.

Return by the Chief Warden, showing the employment of the Prisoners and value of their Earnings during the year ended 31st March, 1897.

Description of Employment.	Daily Average Number of Prisoners (for working days of the year).			Value of Prisoners' Labour.	Total.
	M.	*F.*	Total.	£ s. d.	£ s. d.
In Manufacture :—					
Picking or teasing oakum, hair, &c.,	·49	·44	·93	—	
Shoemaking,	1·18	—	1·18	1 4 6	
Woodcutting,	·09	—	·09	0 3 1	
Total,	1·87	·44	2·21		1 8 1
In Buildings :—					
Carpenters or joiners,	·24	—	·24	2 10 3	
Labourers,	·38	—	·42	17 8 5	
Painters and glaziers,	·38	—	·38	0 17 10	
Whitewashers,	·54	—	·54	0 8 6	
Total,	1·38	—	1·38		20 5 1
In the ordinary service of the Prison :— Cleaning and jobbing work in and about the prison and prison yard and buildings (exclusive of building work of any kind),	·84	·96	1·16	16 14 8	
Pumping water for the service of the prison only,	·68	—	·68	1 11 2	
Repairing all kinds of prison clothing,	·04	·09	·13	3 6 6	
Washing prisoners' clothing,	—	·64	·64	16 18 3	
Total,	1·97	1·85	2·97		41 14 11
Non-effective :—					
Sick,	·04	·04	·08	—	
Under punishment,	·06	—	·06	—	
Unemployed :—					
Awaiting trial,	·08	·04	·12	—	
First class misdemeanants,	·03	—	·06	—	
Total,	·77	·08	·84	—	
Grand Total,	4·75	1·74	5·98	—	67 13 2

OMAGH PRISON.

Return by the Chief Warder, showing the employment of the Prisoners and value of their Earnings during the year ended 31st March, 1897.

Description of Employment.	Daily Average Number of Prisoners (for working days of the year).			Value of Prisoners' Labour.	Total.
	M.	F.	Total.	£ s. d.	£ s. d.
In Manufactures:—					
Picking or beating oakum, hair, &c.,	—	—	·4	—	
Stonebreaking,	1·79	—	1·78	2 0 2	
Woodcutting,	·37	—	·37	2 17 5	
Total . .	1·6	·4	1·9		· · ·
In Buildings:—					
Carpenters or joiners,	·04	—	·04	2 12 8	
Labourers,	·09	—	·02	0 16 5	
Painters and glaziers,	·04	—	·04	1 13 4	
Plasterers,	·02	—	·02	1 0 5	
Smiths,	·01	—	·01	5 25 10	
Whitewashers,	·04	—	·02	0 11 8	
Total , . .	·13	—	·13		· · ·
In the ordinary service of the Prison:—					
Cleaning and jobbing work in and about the prison and prison yard, and buildings (exclusive of building work of any kind),	·75	·18	·93	12 0 6	
Nursing and attending sick prisoners,	·01	·02	·03	0 12 6	
Repairing all kinds of prison clothing,	·07	·12	·12	4 5 3	
Washing prisoners' clothing,	—	·12	·12	3 25 0	
Total	·07	·30	1·06		21 · ·
Non-effective:—					
Sick,	·04	·04	·04	—	
Under punishment,	·03	—	·03	—	
Unemployed:—					
Awaiting trial,	1·70	·22	1·92	—	
Debtors,	·14	—	·14	—	
First class misdemeanants,	·04	—	·04	—	
Others, &c.,	·15	·22	·27	—	
Total,	1·74	·28	2·03	—	
Grand Total, . .	4·04	1·00	5·25	—	25 7 7

WICKLOW PRISON.

Return by the Chief Warder, showing the employment of the Prisoners and value of their Earnings during the year ended 31st March, 1897.

Description of Employment.	Daily Average Number of Prisoners (for working days of the year).			Value of Prisoners' Labour.	Total.
	M.	F.	Total.	£ s. d.	£ s. d.
In Manufactures:—					
Picking or beating oakum, hair, &c.,	·58	—	·58	0 9 2	
Total	·58	—	·58		· · ·

WICKLOW PRISON—*continued.*

Return by the Chief Warder, showing the employment of the Prisoners and value of their Earnings during the year ended 31st March, 1867.

Description of Employment	Daily Average Number of Prisoners (for working days of the year).			Value of Prisoners' Labour.	Total.
	M.	F.	Total.	£ s. d.	£ s. d.
In Buildings:—					
Painters and glaziers, ...	·08	—	·02	0 13 9	
Whitewashers, ...	·10	—	·10	2 16 8	
Total	·13	—	·13		3 5 5
In the ordinary service of the Prison:—					
Cleaning and jobbing work in and about the palace and prison yard, and buildings (exclusive of building work of any kind), . . .	·66	·11	·77	14 19 9	
Pumping water for the service of the prison only, ...	·46	—	·46	8 14 3	
Repairing all kinds of prison clothing,	—	·16	·16	3 6 7	
Washing prisoners' clothing, . .	—	·10	·10	1 17 11	
Woodcutting, ...	·12	—	·12	0 18 5	
Total, ...	1·25	·37	1·62		29 16 9
Non-effectives:—					
Sick, ...	·01	·01	·02	—	
Under punishment, ...	·01	—	·01	—	
Unemployed:—					
Awaiting trial, ...	·40	·02	·42	—	
Total, ...	·42	·20	·62	—	
Grand Total, . .	2·18	·66	2·84	—	33 16 4

RETURN showing employment of Convicts and estimated
value of their Earnings.

CORK MALE PRISON.

No. 1.—VALUE of the Labour of Convicts (as per measured work) for the year
ended 31st March, 1897.

Work.	Daily Average (working days).	No. of Days.		Rate per day earned (per Summary).	Amount.
				£	£ s. d.
Manufactory, ...	99	38	—	·11	0 0 3
Prison Buildings, . . .	1394	4,271	—	1736	318 13 0
Totals, ...	1493	—	4,386	1819	331 13 3
NON-EFFECTIVE.					
Sick, ...	·36	165	—	—	
Under Punishment, . .	91	3	—	—	
Not told off to parties, . .	·466	1	117	—	
		Working days.			
	14·344	x 303	4,366	18·41	314 13 3

No. 2.—SUMMARY of Earnings of the various Trades or Parties for the year
ended 31st March, 1897.

No. of Party,	Employment.	No. of Days.	Average Earnings per Quarter per Day as measured and valued.	Amount.
			d.	£ s. d.
	MANUFACTORY.			
—	Oakum Picking, ...	30	·11	0 0 0
	PRISON BUILDING.			
—	Labouring, ...	2,396.	18·	186 17 0
—	Smithing, ...	520	94·	33 17 2
—	Carpentering, ...	·545	94·	95 · 5 · 0
—	Masons, ...	597	84·	45 24 0
—	Bricklaying, ...	165.	94·	16 6 · 0
—	Whitewashing, ...	7	18·	0 0 0
	Total, ...			336 15 0

RETURN showing employment of Convicts and estimated
value of their Earnings—*continued.*

MARYBOROUGH CONVICT PRISON.

No. 1.—VALUE of the Labour of Convicts (as per measured work) for the
year ended 31st March, 1897.

Work.	Daily Average (Working Days).	Number of Days.	Rate per day earned (= Summary).	Amount.
			d.	£ s. d.
Manufactory, . .	6·44	1,849	17·	132 1 1
Prison Buildings, . .	31·76	8,873	16·23	574 15 4
Prison Employment, . .	342	—	11,472	10·90	512 14 5
	332	—	10,047	12·	503 17 5
Totals, . . .	71·4	—	21,012	14·6	1,314 15 4
NON-EFFECTIVE.				
Under Punishment, . .	·9	—	61	—
Escaped from Labour on Medical grounds.	17·	—	5,841	—
Grand Totals, . .	63·9 × 603 = 76,891		13·17	1,315 15 4

No. 2.—SUMMARY of Earnings of the various Trades or Parties, for the year
ended 31st March, 1897.

No. of Party.	Employment.	No. of Days.	Average Earnings per Convict per Day as increased and valued.	Amount.
	MANUFACTORY.		*d.*	£ s. d.
—	Tailoring, ...	1,441	17·	102 8 9
—	Shoemaking, . . .	408	17·	44 11 4
		1,849	17·	132 1 1
	PRISON BUILDINGS.			
—	Carpenters, ...	678	24·	67 12 0
—	Smithing, ...	127	24·	12 9 0
—	Labourers, . . .	8,068	14·	476 3 4
		8,873	16·23	674 15 4
	PRISON EMPLOYMENT.			
—	Labourers, ...	3,619	12·	160 11 4
—	Gardening, ...	2,748	12·	137 8 0
—	Cleaning Prison, . .	2,131	13·	106 1 0
—	Repairing Clothing and Bedding,	1,055	11·	53 15 4
—	Washing Clothing and Bedding,	606	13·	30 0 4
—	Cooking, ...	849	13·	45 0 0
		10,957	12·	522 15 0

RETURN showing employment of Convicts and estimated
value of their Earnings—*continued.*

MOUNTJOY CONVICT PRISON.

No. 1.—VALUE of the Labour of Convicts (as per measured work), for the
year ended 31st March, 1897.

Work.	Daily Average (working days.)	No. of Days.	Rate per day earned (see Summary).	Amount.
			d.	*£ s. d.*
Manufactory.	171·659	51,892·277	11·92	2,589 0 2
Prison Buildings.	57·897	11,316·981	18·11	892 0 6
				8,484 0 2
Prison Employment.	28·907	10,824·391	13·19	597 18 5
Totals.	248·984	73,826·842	18·72	4,041 18 9
NON-EFFECTIVE.				
Sick.	7·784	2,884·312		
Not told off in parties.	2·605	977·185		3,315·697
		Working days.		
Grand Totals.	254·583	77,132·946	12·7	4,041 18 9

No. 2.—SUMMARY of Earnings of the various Trades or Parties, for the year
ended 31st March, 1897.

No. of Party.	Employment.	No. of Days.	Average Earnings per Convict per Day as measured and valued.	Amount
			d.	*£ s. d.*
	PRISON BUILDINGS.			
—	Labouring,	4,227·848	18·	848 8 7
—	Smithing,	740·855	24·	74 1 8
—	Masons,	102·804	24·	10 6 8
—	Painting,	1,764·419	28·8	189 11 8
—	Whitewashing,	760·834	12·	37 16 10
—	Plastering,	208·940	24·	20 18 11
—	Carpentering,	3,008·982	21·	300 12 5
		11,316·981	18·14	892 0 6
	PRISON EMPLOYMENT.			
—	Cleaning,	4,557·443	12·	227 17 8
—	Store Porters,	1,008·943	12·	50 3 3
—	Stokers,	181·903	12·	10 18 4
—	Cooks,	1,880·355	18·6	142·75 3
—	Washing,	2,782·117	12·	138 18 8
—	Bookbinding,	815·317	24·	34 10 10
		10,824·391	13·50	597 18 1
	MANUFACTORY.			
—	Tailoring,	14,858·024	18·8	1,318 8 8
—	Shoemaking,	13,584·808	11·6	350 18 5
—	Oakum Picking,	1,829·844	3·0	4 4 7
—	Matmaking,	11,827·970	1·8	76 2 7
—	Baking,	1,768·960	13·6	133 1 8
—	Carpentering,	600·	16·8	62 12 7
—	Cutting Firewood,	4,735·60	8·48	124 0 4
—	Tinsmithing,	908·728	24·	39 11 5
		51,892·277	11·09	2,589 0 2

RETURN showing employment of Convicts and estimated
value of their Earnings—*continued.*

GRANGEGORMAN CONVICT PRISON.

No. 1.—VALUE of the Labour of Convicts (as per measured work) for the
year ended 31st March, 1897.

Work.	Daily Average (working days).	No. of Days.		Rate per day earned (see Summary).	Amount.
				d.	£ s. d.
Manufactory, . . .	19·53	5,017·49	—	10·	249 11 6
Prison employment, ; .	7·93	2,290·76	—	10·41	165 2 5
Totals, .	27·45	—	8,317·25	11·95	414 13 7
NON-EFFECTIVE.					
Punishment, . .	·06	15·18	—	—	—
Nursing Children, &c., .	1·13	831·25	—	—	—
Hospital, . . .	4·27	1,263·51	1,621·06	—	—
		Working days.		Average earnings	
				d.	
Grand Totals. .	82·96	× 363 =	8,838·50	10·91	414 13 7

No. 2.—SUMMARY of the Earnings of the various Trades or Parties, for the
year ended 31st March, 1897.

No. of Party.	Employment.	No. of Days.	Average Earnings per Convict per Day as measured and valued.	Amount.
	MANUFACTORY.		d.	£ s. d.
—	Knitting and Needlework. .	5,017·99	10·	249 11 6
	PRISON EMPLOYMENT.			
—	Cooking for Prisoners, . .	1,212·	22·	114 3 6
—	Cleaning Prison, ...	1,197·76	10·6	51 18 3
		2,889·76	16·91	165 1 5

Daily Average Number of Convicts in Custody during the Year . . 85·99
Percentage on Prison Population Working, ... 82·69
Do. do. do. Sick and Nursing Children, . . 16·23
Do. do. do. In Punishment, ... ·18

TABLE XXV.—NUMBER of queries as to Prisoners in Custody awaiting Trial, received from Prisons and Police during each of the following years, showing the per-centage known :—

YEAR.	Queries received from		Per-centage known.	
	Prisons.	Police.	Prisons.	Police.
1870a.	—	—	—	—
1871b.	47	27	31·9	15·
1872,	89	40	36·36	35·
1873,	131	24	37·08	46·
1874,	133	42	40·6	38·09
1875,	154	32	33·54	15·62
1876,	130	23	26·13	8·
1877,	82	24	19·56	29·
1878,	73	28	26·	25·
1879,	57	35	21·	8·6
1880,	133	75	54·9	1·07
1880–81,	118	52	60·8	5·
1881–82,	140	13	79·3	7·7
1882–83,	99	15	81·9	6·6
1883–84,	96	3	89·3	—
1884–85,	92	6	83·7	50·
1885–86,	98	9	93·	11·
1886–87,	101	5	87·	40·
1887–88,	94	2	91·3	100·
1888–89,	94	—	94·6	—
1889–90,	89	1	98·5	—
1890–91,	98	5	96·	20·
1891–92,	75	—	96·6	—
1892–93,	74	5	94·6	·60
1893–94,	71	1	97·	—
1894–95,	89	—	97·9	—
1895,	66	—	93·4	—
1896,	108	—	96·29	—

a. No record kept.   b. Commencing August, 1871.

TABLE XXVI—NUMBER of habitual criminals and discharged convicts registered in :

Year.	No.	Year.	No.
1870,	907	1884–85,	172
1871,	1,058	1885–86,	206
1872,	840	1886–87,	250
1873,	1,116	1887–88,	145
1874,	1,062	1888–89,	150
1875,	986	1889–90,	131
1876,	984	1890–91,	123
1877,	809	1891–92,	144
1878,	272	1892–93,	140
1879,	363	1893–94,	126
1880–81,	285	1894–95,	161
1881–82,	924	1895,	180
1882–83,	169	1896,	167
1883–84,	164		

TABLE XXVIII.—Return showing the Expenditure of each Convict and Maintenance in the year

HEADS OF SERVICE.	Totals.	Mountjoy.
Daily average number of prisoners (including Minor Prisons and Bridewells).	{ MALES, 2,110 } { FEMALES, 307 } Total, 2,517	M. 542
A.—COST OF STAFF.		
Pay and allowances of officers, including uniforms, &c., and fine fund.	64,540 2 1	£ s. d. 31,540 6 8
Average annual charge per prisoner,	10 10 1	10 7 6
B.—MAINTENANCE OF PRISONERS.		
Victualling for prisoners,	16,360 4 11	4,773 7 5
Medicines, surgical instruments, &c.	470 5 3	150 1 0
Fuel, light, and water,	6,540 15 3	2,301 3 4
Soap, scouring and cleaning articles,	626 11 5	110 11 7
Clothing for prisoners,	3,557 8 7	780 6 4
Bedding for prisoners,	641 4 10	167 3 4
Furniture, kitchen utensils, crockery, &c.	410 8 8	77 6 3
Total expenses of Maintenance,	28,538 14 7	7,945 6 10
Average annual charge per prisoner,	10 10 4	13 13 1

HEADS OF SERVICE.	Armagh.	Belfast.	Castlebar.
Daily average number of prisoners (including Minor Prisons and Bridewells).	{ M. 62 } { F. 94 }	{ M. 776 } { F. 87 }	{ M. 80 } { F. 9 }

and Local Prison (including Minor Prisons and Bridewells) for Staff
ended 31st March, 1897.

Grangegorman.	Maryborough.	HEADS OF SERVICE.
v. 815	m. 86	Daily average number of prisoners (including Minor Prisons and Bridewells).
		A.—COST OF STAFF.
£ s. d.	£ s. d.	
8,367 8 10	3,176 19 0	Pay and allowances of officers, including uniforms, &c., and Sun fund.
16 13 7	8f 16 10	Average annual charge per prisoner.
		B.—MAINTENANCE OF PRISONERS.

Table XXVIII—Return showing the Expenditure of each Convict
and Maintenance in the year

HEADS OF SERVICE.	Dundalk.	Galway.	Kilkenny.
Daily average number of prisoners (including Minor Prisons and Bridewells.	{M. 6" {P. 8	M. 84} P. 14}	M. 7s
A.—COST OF STAFF.	£ s. d.	£ s. d.	£ s. d.
Pay and allowances of officers, including uniforms, &c., and bar fund.	1,438 9 11	1,619 4 9	2,031 10 2
Average annual charge per prisoner, .	22 7 9	71 1 7	26 4 9
B.—MAINTENANCE OF PRISONERS.			
Victualling for prisoners, ...	339 1 6	648 19 6	339 19 2
Medicines, surgical instruments. &c.,	16 10 9	10 9 1	11 4 4
Fuel, light, and water, ...	307 9 11	231 17 7	314 17 2
Soap, scouring and cleaning articles, .	16 6 6	61 7 9	79 19 9
Clothing for prisoners, ...	92 7 11	61 4 6	61 9 3
Bedding for prisoners, ...	10 19 5	8 18 10	53 6 6
Furniture, kitchen utensils, crockery, &c.,	31 16 6	41 17 9	16 16 9
Total expenses of Maintenance,	762 11 10	755 16 0	875 15 3
Average annual charge per prisoner, .	10 14 6	16 9 0	11 19 6

HEADS OF SERVICE.	Sligo.	Tralee.
Daily average number of prisoners (including Minor Prisons and Bridewells).	{M. 61 {P. 19	M. 44} P. 6}
A.—COST OF STAFF.	£ s. d.	£ s. d.
Pay and allowances of officers, including uniforms, &c., and pay fund.	1,396 13 11	1,941 9 9
Average annual charge per prisoner, ...	26 19 7	34 16 9
B.—MAINTENANCE OF PRISONERS.		
Victualling for prisoners, ...	343 1 9	284 9 3
Medicines, surgical instruments, &c., . . .	31 4 4	7 9 7
Fuel, light, and water, ...	330 11 11	233 14 9
Soap, scouring and cleaning articles, . . .	11 14 9	19 1 9
Clothing for prisoners, ...	71 14 4	39 9 9
Bedding for prisoners, ...	17 11 3	16 19 3
Furniture, kitchen utensils, crockery, &c., . .	9 4 9	13 8 10
Total expenses of Maintenance, . . .	787 6 0	673 1 6
Average annual charge per prisoner, . . :	10 17 1	11 9 3

and Local Prison (including Minor Prisons and Bridewells) for Staff
ending 31st March, 1897—*continued.*

Kilmainham.	Limerick, Male.	Limerick, Female.	Londonderry.	HEADS OF SERVICE.
M. 190	M. 97	F. 41	{ M. 80 / F. 84 }	Daily average number of prisoners (including Minor Prisons and Bridewells).
				A.—COST OF STAFF.
£ s. d. 6,673 4 1	£ s. d. 1,903 10 4	£ s. d. 744 16' 0	£ s. d. 9,441 15 1	Pay and allowances of officers, including uniforms, &c., and Con fund.
31 7 8	90 9 1	18 0'11	80 5 4	Average annual charge per prisoner.
				B.—MAINTENANCE OF PRISONERS.
763 13 8	850 6 3	726 5 2	577 5 1	Victualling for prisoners.
18 21 10	6 1 2	9 13'10	91 16 8	Medicine, surgical instruments, &c.
399 0 0	244 4 7	766 9'16	130 9 8	Fuel, light, and water.
94 9 9	15 16 11	41 11 11	37 10 4	Soap, scouring and cleaning articles.
154 11 7	19 14 4	43 5' 6	100 13 8	Clothing for prisoners.
48 1 8	9 14 11	8 1 2	8 4 8	Bedding for prisoners.
35 13 4	98 18 3	9 13 8	98 18 8	Furniture, kitchen utensils, crockery, &c.
1,583 9 0	941 4 4	608 8 1	1,148 16 8	Total expenses of Maintenance.
8 1 7	9 14 0	15 4 1	10 8 9	Average annual charge per prisoner.

Tullamore.	Waterford.	Wexford.	HEADS OF SERVICE.
{ M. 99 / F. 19 }	{ M. 93 / F. 40 }	{ M. 61 / F. 6 }	Daily average number of prisoners (including Minor Prisons and Bridewells).
			A.—COST OF STAFF.
£ s. d. 1,979 5 10	£ s. d. 4,401 4 9	£ s. d. 1,913 10 1	Pay and allowances of officers, including uniforms, &c., and Con fund.
18 10 0	81 16 1	13 1 7	Average annual charge per prisoner.
			B.—MAINTENANCE OF PRISONERS.
841 13 8	914 9 11	990 17 8	Victualling for prisoners.
16 5 8	14 5 9	8 9 10	Medicine, surgical instruments, &c.
884 7 8	898 9 11	149 8 9	Fuel, light, and water.
19 17 2	38 4 7	9 6 1	Soap, scouring and cleaning articles.
119 11 8	104 17 8	88 9 10	Clothing for prisoners.
46 17 7	91 13 8	6 11 0	Bedding for prisoners.
84 18 5	13 4 4	6 1 7	Furniture, kitchen utensils, crockery, &c.
1,109 18 0	783 1 8	680 16 8	Total expenses of Maintenance.
11 4 8	11 10 8	11 1 4	Average annual charge per prisoner.

H

TABLE XXIX.—C. Expenses of Convict and Local Prisons, other than for Staff and Maintenance, in the year ended 31st March, 1897.

HEADS OF SERVICE.	TOTALS.
	£ s. d.
Gratuities to prisoners (including grant to Discharged Prisoners' Aid Societys), ...	1,542 1 1
Escort and conveyance of prisoners, ...	4,513 13 4
New buildings and alterations, ...	1,628 4 7
Ordinary repairs of buildings, ...	6,545 9 13
Rent, ...	694 15 3
Incidental expenses (including travelling and removal expenses of officers), ...	1,593 14 9
Maintenance of children of female prisoners, . . .	9 19 7
Washing for public departments, ...	13 1 3
Total of other expenses, ...	17,144 4 11
Do. exclusive of new buildings and alterations and washing for public departments, ...	15,507 19 3
Average annual charge per prisoner, ...	9 11 4

SUMMARY OF A, B, AND C.

REGULATIONS made by the LORDS JUSTICES of IRELAND under the PENAL SERVITUDE ACT, 1891, Sections 8 and 9, for the MEASURING and PHOTOGRAPHING of PRISONERS.

1. Subject as hereinafter mentioned, a criminal prisoner may be photographed and measured at any time during his imprisonment.

2. He shall be photographed either in the dress of the prison, or in the dress he wore at the time of his arrest or trial, or in any other dress suitable to his ostensible position and occupation in life.

The photograph to be taken shall include a photograph of the full face, and a photograph of the true profile of the prisoner.

3. The measurements to be taken may include :—

The length and breadth of the head.
The length and breadth of the face.
The length and breadth of the ears.
The length of either foot.
The length of the fingers of either hand.
The length of the cubit and hand, either right or left.
The span of the arms.
The prisoner's height when standing.
The prisoner's height when sitting.
The size and relative position of every scar and distinctive mark upon any part of the body.

The external filament of the fingers and thumbs of both hands to be taken by pressing them, first upon an inked plate, and then upon paper or cardboard, so as to leave a clear print of the skin surface.

4. An untried criminal prisoner shall not be photographed or measured while in prison save by order of the Lord Lieutenant or upon an application in writing signed by an officer of police of not lower rank than District Inspector, and approved by a Justice of the Peace, or in the Metropolitan Police District by the Commissioner or Assistant Commissioner of Police, and all such applications shall set forth that from the character of the offence with which the prisoner is charged, or for other reasons, there are grounds for suspecting that he has been previously convicted, or has been engaged in crime, or that from any other cause his photograph and measurements are required for the purposes of justice.

5. When an untried prisoner, who has not been previously convicted of crime, shall have been photographed and measured under the preceding regulation, if he be discharged by the Magistrate or acquitted upon his trial, all photographs (both negatives and copies), finger print impressions, and records of measurements so taken, shall be forthwith destroyed, or handed over to the prisoner.

ROBERTS.

HEDGES EYRE CHATTERTON.

DUBLIN CASTLE,
30th March, 1897

REPORTS BY SUPERIOR OFFICERS OF CONVICT PRISONS.

MARYBOROUGH CONVICT PRISONS.

GOVERNOR'S REPORT.

H. M. Convict Prison, Maryborough,
May 1st, 1897.

Sir,—I have the honour to submit my report on the condition and incidents of this prison during the year ended 31st March, 1897, as required by Rule 185. The statistical returns for the calendar year have been forwarded to Board's Office on 11th February as directed.

The conduct of the subordinate officers has been very satisfactory. Late Chief Warder John Barrett, after 33 years service, retired on potatoes, and although the conditions as regards timely tilling were very unfavourable yet the crop was good and abundant, especially as regards the quality known as "Bounties of Bute," which were fully three times more prolific than Champion, sown side by side. I again sprayed the potatoes but your with a mixture of sulphate of copper and lime, with very favourable results. I had no blight either whilst the potatoes were growing or on the tubers afterwards. As already stated, I was only able to have two acres tilled last year, a portion was under meadow, and remainder not for grazing, the final results being a saving of about £80 on the year's transactions, but not including any of the expenses in connection with purchase, or the building of the wall. The draining of the farm has progressed most satisfactorily, and this year a very large proportion of it will be under crops of potatoes and vegetables. I have reason to believe that profit was not a prevailing force by which the Board was influenced in acquiring this farm, but rather to afford healthful, useful and educational employment for convicts, enabling them to cultivate habits of industry, and to acquire a knowledge of work, by which they can, if so disposed, live honestly after their discharge from prison, which is the most difficult and critical period in the life of the criminal. I believe that these objects will be attended with a large measure of success, for it is certain that even city reared criminals take a very great interest in the draining, cultivation, and cropping of the land, and (as one of the Chaplains remarks in his report) the quantity and quality of the work produced is the surprise of the inhabitants of the locality.

The necessary repairs to prison buildings have been maintained.

The conduct of the prisoners in the Intermediate Class has been most satisfactory. Previous to their discharge I communicate with the clergymen of the districts in which they are respectively about to reside, requesting that everything convenient might be done in furtherance of their desire to obtain employment and the means of living honestly; these efforts I think are laudable, are in accordance with the desire of the Board, and are instrumental to good.

The invalid prisoners when not totally incapacitated, and when fit for any work, have been suitably employed at shoemaking, tailoring, cooking, cleaning prison, and tilling garden inside the prison walls. Their conduct has been very good, the cases of misconduct being very few and slight.

The prisoners of the invalid class are each and all suffering from some form of disease, yet their health has been maintained at a high standard; one death has occurred in this class from syncope, or failure of heart action, since the statistical reports have been forwarded.

There have been no escapes, nor attempts to escape, during the year.

The Chaplains have been zealous and attentive, willingly co-operating in every effort for the improvement and for the reformation of the convicts whilst in prison, and their welfare after discharge.

The morning and evening schools continue to be conducted as in have been complied with to the best of my knowledge and belief, except in such cases as have been specially reported to the Board.

The Visiting Committee visited the prison on 8th April, 13th May, 10th June, 8th July, 13th August, 9th September, 14th October, 11th November, 9th December, 1896; 13th January, 10th February, and 10th March, 1897. I take the liberty to acknowledge with feelings of gratitude the valuable assistance and advice always willingly given by them in the interests of the prison and for the benefit of the prisoners whenever considered desirable.

I have the honour to be, Sir,

Your obedient servant,

JOHN CORBIN, Governor.

To the Chairman,
General Prisons Board,
Dublin Castle.

PROTESTANT EPISCOPALIAN CHAPLAIN'S REPORT.

Portlaois, Maryborough,
30th April, 1897.

SIR,—The services on the Lord's Day were during the last twelve months very regularly attended by all the Protestant prisoners. I have for some time visited the men in their cells instead of holding a service on Wednesdays. Some prisoners objected to having to attend these week-day services, and as all who were registered as members of the Church of Ireland were obliged to attend them, some in consequence applied for leave to change their religion, most to join the Presbyterian Church, one, Convict F, first joined the Presbyterians, and on re-committal to prison, after a very short absence, he had himself registered a Jew.

The attendance of the prisoners under my care at the evening school has been satisfactory. To men whose education was altogether or greatly neglected, this school is a considerable advantage.

I received during the year, in the discharge of my duties, from the intern officers, every assistance in their power to render.

I have the honour to be, Sir,

Your obedient servant,

ROBT. L. EVES,
Church of Ireland Chaplain.

The Chairman, General Prisons Board.

ROMAN CATHOLIC CHAPLAIN'S REPORT.

Maryboro',
19th April, 1897.

SIR,—I have much pleasure in giving a satisfactory report of the Maryboro' Prison for the past year. The chaplains have, I think, received fewer complaints from the prisoners of their treatment than during any other year since my arrival in Maryboro'. I think, also, that notwithstanding the great increase in numbers the discipline has been equally good. The progress in the educational department has also been satisfactory. I am very proud that my suggestion (often made) about acquiring some land adjoining the prison has been carried out. It will, I hope, be of the greatest advantage to the prisoners, in body and mind, to have them working on this farm in place of being enclosed within the dismal walls of the prison. The officials are pushing on the work with great energy, and it is admired by every passer-by.

I remain, your most obedient servant,

A. PHELAN, P.P.

To the Chairman of Prisons Board.

MEDICAL OFFICERS' REPORT.

H. M. Convict Prison, Maryboro'

17th April, 1897.

Sir,—We have the honour to submit our annual report on the health of the officers and prisoners, and the sanitary condition of this prison for the year ending the 31st March, 1897.

During the year no serious illness occurred to any member of the staff. Chief Warder Barrow, found to be physically unfit for duty—owing to defective vision—was retired on pension.

We have to record but one death (which occurred since furnishing our yearly statistics) that of an invalid class prisoner.

Influenza was prevalent during January and February this year, but it was of a mild character, leaving no ill effects after it.

The labour class prisoners maintained throughout the year a high standard of health. This, no doubt, was largely due to their employment—farm work—being healthy, and particularly suitable to the constitution of the average convict.

The sanitary condition of the prison and buildings continues satisfactory ; the water supply good in quality, and abundant.

Again we have the pleasure of placing on record our appreciation of the facilities and support afforded to us at all times in the discharge of our duties by the Governor and the staff under his control.

We have the honour to be, Sir,

Your obedient servants,

J. I. KINSELLA,
Physician, Surgeon, and L.M., Resident Medical Officer.

D. B. JACOB, M.D.,
Consulting and Visiting Physician.

MOUNTJOY MALE CONVICT PRISON.

GOVERNOR'S REPORT.

Mountjoy Prison,
April, 1897.

Sir,—I have the honour to report for the year ended 31st March, 1897, on the convict portion of Mountjoy Prison.

The subordinate officers have been generally well conducted, attentive, and diligent; cases of negligence or inattention to rules or duties, on their part, have been few and not serious. Only two cases occurred during the year that were not within my powers to deal with, and these were disposed of by the Board. The Chief and Principal Warders have performed their duties zealously and judiciously. The changes on the staff during the year were as follows:—A Principal Warder and a first-class Warder were discharged on pension, and others promoted in their stead, one Principal Warder was promoted to be Chief Warder at Maryboro' Prison. One Principal Warder and six Warders were removed to Maryboro' Prison, one Warder was transferred to the local service at his own request, and four Warders were transferred from the local to the convict staff.

The convicts have, in general, been well-conducted and industrious, and many of them have quickly become proficient at trades and occupations of which they previously had no knowledge. Punishments for prison offences have not been many, and it has not been necessary even to reprimand the great majority of the convicts in custody during the year. The rules are fully explained to all on entering the prison, and the vast majority do not need pressure or compulsion to ensure compliance.

There were 292 convicts in custody at Mountjoy Prison on 1st April, 1896; 68 were received during the year under now sentences, 30 were received on forfeiture or revocation of licences, one was returned from the Criminal Asylum, and seven from Maryboro' Prison. There were 96 convicts removed to Maryboro' Prison during the year (63 of these were for employment on a newly acquired farm, and they were specially selected as regards conduct, disposition, capacity for outdoor labour, and suitability for employment with comparative safety outside the prison), four were removed to Cork Male Prison for work there, six to the Criminal Asylum, 88 were released on licence, and four discharged absolutely, leaving only 210 in custody here on the 31st March, 1897.

The greater part of the outdoor labour for convicts at Mountjoy Prison ceased on the completion of twenty-three houses outside the prison for married warders, at the close of April, 1896, but this caused no inconvenience, as the subsequent removals to Maryboro' Prison disposed of all those not required for the necessary indoor trades, gardening, cleaning, and the maintenance and repairs of the extensive prison buildings comprising the convict and local prisons, workshops, &c., and the numerous residential buildings attached thereto, sixty of which are outside the prison walls. All have been kept in good repair by convict labour.

Uniform and boots for the staffs of most of the Irish prisons continue to be made by the convicts at Mountjoy, as well as clothing and foot wear for prisoners in nearly all Irish prisons, carpentry-work, smith-work, tin-work, coopering, &c., are also done here for other prisons, as required. Convicts incapable of learning trades, or of becoming proficient at them, are employed at mat-making and wood-chopping, chiefly for public departments. Baking bread for all the Dublin prisons continues to be done advantageously at Mountjoy by convict labour.

There has not been any escape or attempt to escape during the year.

The Medical Officer and his assistant have been unremitting in their attention to the health of both officers and prisoners.

The Chaplains have attended regularly, and all have shown much anxiety for the welfare of the convicts after discharge, as well as for their spiritual interests and reformation while in prison.

The Schoolmasters have been painstaking and attentive, and the school records show satisfactory results. The Schoolmasters also act as librarians for the convicts' library, and they change books daily during the dinner hour, as required.

I certify that the rules laid down for the government of the prison have been complied with, except in such cases as have been reported to or brought to the notice of the General Prisons Board.

I have the honour to be, Sir,

Your most obedient servant,

Geo. Sheehan, Governor.

The Chairman, General Prisons Board.

PROTESTANT EPISCOPALIAN CHAPLAIN'S REPORT.

H. M. Prison, Mountjoy,
April 23, 1897.

Sir,—In submitting my Report for the past twelve months, I am happy to be able to speak very favourably of those committed to my charge. There has been no serious infringement of discipline, while the conduct at Divine Service, and during religious instruction, both on Sundays and week days, has been good.

I am glad to find that some of those who have entered prison, quite, or nearly so, illiterate, become, by diligence and attention at the school, able to read and write, and that they acquire a certain amount of knowledge in other branches of secular education. Such proficiency offers valuable opportunities for the perusal of the Sacred Scriptures and books of devotion furnished to them in their cells.

We have had scarcely any sickness during the year; but my visits to the fine hospital confirm previous experience in regard of the important factor which the infirmary supplies towards the working of the gaol.

I desire thankfully to record the unremitting exertions of Mr. H. P. Goodbody, the Honorary Secretary of our Prisoner's Aid Society, and also to acknowledge my obligations to the Governor and the entire staff for ready co-operation in the discharge of my responsible duties.

I have the honour, Sir, to remain

Your obedient servant,

John H. MacMahon, M.A., LL.D.,

Protestant Chaplain.

To the Chairman of the General Prisons Board.

ROMAN CATHOLIC CHAPLAINS' REPORT.

Mountjoy Prison, June, 1897.

Sir,—In submitting our report for the year ended March, 1897, it gives us much pleasure to bear testimony to the satisfactory condition of the prisoners under our charge. They were, during the year, very attentive to their various religious duties. Whilst in the Church their demeanour was all that could be desired, and they approached the sacraments regularly, with a few exceptions.

In our daily intercourse with them through the prison, we invariably found them cheerful and agreeable.

The general discipline of the prison was, we are of opinion, excellent in every department.

We beg to thank the Governor, the Medical Officer, and the other officials of the prison, for their kindness to us on all occasions, and for the assistance they gave us in the discharge of our duties.

We have the honour to remain, Sir, your obedient servants,

M. WALSH, R.C.C.

T. O'DONNELL, Asst. R.C.C.

PRESBYTERIAN CHAPLAIN'S REPORT.

Mountjoy Convict Prison,
April 14, 1897.

Sir,—I can speak in terms of the highest praise of the conduct of the prisoners under my care in relation to their respectful attention to religious instruction. Their general conduct has also been exceptionally good, cases of punishment having been rare throughout the year. Two years ago I thought it advisable to administer the Sacrament of the Lord's Supper to those prisoners who desired it, and have done so twice a year since. It had not been done heretofore, I believe, and those who joined in the celebration seemed to be helped and benefited. The number of Presbyterian convicts is rapidly decreasing year by year, and there are fewer now, I believe, than at any past time.

Faithfully,
J. C. JOHNSTON,
Presbyterian Chaplain.

To the Chairman of H. M.'s General Prisons Board.

MEDICAL OFFICER'S REPORT.

Mountjoy Convict Prison,
31st March, 1897.

Sir,—I have the honour to submit the annual report on the health of the officers and convicts, and on the general sanitary state of this prison with the usual medical statistics for the year ended 31st December last.

During the year there were thirty-eight warders treated in hospital—chiefly for influenza, bronchitis, rheumatism, and two cases of typhoid fever. One principal warder and one first-class warder were discharged the service on medical grounds. There was no death.

There were seventeen convicts in hospital on the 1st January, 1896, and 140 were admitted during the year. The chief ailments were influenza, bronchitis, dyspepsia, rheumatism, and diarrhœa. Of those in hospital:—eight were transferred to the invalid prison, three were removed to the Criminal Lunatic Asylum, one was discharged from prison on medical grounds, and one died from pneumonia.

Nothing occurred during the year demanding any special reference. The health of the officers and prisoners was generally good, and the sanitary arrangements of the prison were carefully attended to.

I have the honour to be, Sir,
Your obedient servant,
P. O'KEEFFE, M.D.,
Medical Officer.

The Chairman, General Prisons Board,
Dublin Castle.

GRANGEGORMAN FEMALE CONVICT PRISON.

SUPERINTENDENT'S REPORT.

H. M. Prison, Grangegorman,
1st May, 1897.

Sir,—I have the honour to submit my annual report on the Convict Prison for the year ended 31st March, 1897, with statistical returns.

The subordinate officers have been well conducted and attentive to their duties during the year.

The prisoners' conduct has been most satisfactory, the number punished for offences against prison discipline, being exceptionally small.

The convicts are principally employed in laundry work, knitting and sewing, also whitewashing, painting, and gardening. Three have been constantly employed in the kitchen, cooking for convict and local prisoners.

The school has been conducted, as usual, with most satisfactory results.

I certify that the Rules laid down for the government of the prison have been adhered to, except in such cases as have been brought to the notice of the General Prisons Board.

I have the honour to be, Sir,
Your obedient servant,
CATHERINE J. M'CARTHY,
Superintendent.

PROTESTANT EPISCOPALIAN CHAPLAIN'S REPORT.

H. M. Convict Prison, Grangegorman,
31st May, 1897.

Sir,—I have no change to report in regard to the Convicts under my charge; two of them will be discharged during the year. One is unusually well educated, and very intelligent, the others are of a low type, and extremely ignorant—one of them, however, has made persevering efforts in learning to read.

The discipline of the prison is in my opinion well maintained, and I have at all times received from the officers consideration and help in carrying out my duties as Chaplain.

I am yours faithfully,
HENRY HOGAN,
Chaplain.

To the Chairman of the
General Prisons Board.

ROMAN CATHOLIC CHAPLAIN'S REPORT.

Grangegorman Prison,
June 2nd, 1897.

Sir,—I have the honour to submit my report for the year ended March 31st.

The prisoners have been well conducted, and with few exceptions very attentive to their religious duties.

I beg to repeat the view I expressed in my report of last year as to the necessity of a five years' sentence for *habitual offenders*—that is, for those women who after five or six short convictions manifest an inward propensity for crime; and I beg again to refer to the statistics read at the Royal Commission of 1883 in reference to the amount of good effected among such prisoners in Golden Bridge Refuge, where they were allowed to remain in comparative freedom for the last sixteen months of their sentence.

I wish also to point out that prisoners (especially females) discharged from Irish prisons are in a very different position from prisoners discharged in England. In England it is by no means difficult for a well-conducted woman on discharge to procure a respectable situation; in Ireland it is practically an impossibility.

I must add too, that in my opinion, a sentence of five years for habitual female offenders (as I have defined an "habitual offender") in Ireland is the most merciful, as by no shorter sentence are our prisoners enabled, no matter how great may be their industry or how good their conduct, to earn as much as would be sufficient to take them out of the country.

I have the honour to be, Sir,
Your obedient servant,
J. ANDERSON,
R. C. Chaplain.

PRESBYTERIAN CHAPLAIN'S REPORT.

Grangegorman Prison,
15/4/97.

Sir,—There is only one Presbyterian female convict. She had passed, I understand, a considerable portion of her life in a lunatic asylum before her committal to prison. She is very tractable and quiet as a rule; but her mind seems still unsettled.

Faithfully,

J. C. JOHNSTON

Presbyterian Chaplain.

The Chairman,
H. M.'s Prisons Board.

MEDICAL OFFICER'S REPORT.

H. M. Prison, Grangegorman,
3rd June, 1897.

Sir,—I have the honour to lay before you my Report for the year ended 31st March, 1897, together with the usual medical statistics.

The absence of mortality and the relatively small number of cases of serious illness tend to show that the sanitary condition of the prison leaves nothing to be desired.

I have the honour to be, Sir,

Your obedient servant,

R. C. DOWNALL, M.B.

www.ingramcontent.com/pod-product-compliance
Lightning Source LLC
Chambersburg PA
CBHW032016010726
47493CB00007B/2431